The Tomorrow People

THE RAMESES CONNECTION

Nigel Robinson

sapling

First published in the UK 1995 by Sapling, an imprint of
BOXTREE LIMITED
Broadwall House, 21 Broadwall, London SE1 9PL

10 9 8 7 6 5 4 3 2 1

Text based on THE TOMORROW PEOPLE, a Tetra Films Production in Association with Thames Television Ltd and Nickelodeon
Executive Producer – Roger Price
Producer – Alan Horrox
Director – Roger Gartland

Original script for THE RAMESES CONNECTION by Grant Cathro

Front cover photograph: Adam (Kristian Schmid), Ami (Naomie Harris) and Megabyte (Christian Tessier)
Back cover photographs: Rameses (Christopher Lee), Mrs Motherwell (Sarah Flind), Rupert Short (Christopher Brand), Millicent (Elizabeth Spriggs) and Red Rainwear (Anthony O'Donnell)

ISBN: 0 7522 0647 8

Typeset in Galliard by SX Composing Ltd., Rayleigh, Essex
Printed and bound by Cox & Wyman, Reading, Berkshire

A CIP catalogue entry is available from the British Library

The Tomorrow People

THE RAMESES CONNECTION

Chapter One

Over Four Thousand Years Ago

The sinking sun blistered down on the mighty city of Akhetaton, turning the endless desert sands a deep red, the colour of human blood. It was that witching hour, that no-man's time between daytime and night, between the light and the dark. Sinister creatures were abroad at this time, so the old wise-women sheltering by the palace walls said, demons and imps from the dawn of time, servants of the devil-god Set. It was a time when the forces of evil were at their strongest; it was a time when children died.

Racing into the enclosed palace gardens there came a young man, no more than eighteen years of age. He was dressed in a simple loincloth, but the golden chains around his neck marked him out as the Pharaoh, ruler of all Egypt, and direct descendant of the sun-god Ra. He was the mightiest of all his people, having the power of life or death over each and every one of his subjects; and yet he was in fear for his life.

With wide, frightened eyes, he looked around the

garden, spying into the shadows, checking that he was alone. A soft breeze rustled through the trees and ornamental palms; in the centre of the gardens, crystal-clear water tinkled out of an elaborately carved stone fountain.

He glanced up at the high walls which surrounded the gardens, and tensed. For a second, he thought he saw someone crouching on top of the wall – a squat figure, no more than three feet high, staring down at him like a malevolent dwarf. Then he blinked and, in a blur of red, the creature was gone – if, indeed, it had been there in the first place.

The young Pharaoh wiped his brow which was glistening with a thin sheen of cold sweat. The hand that he has raised was trembling, and his heart was pounding so hard that he swore it would burst out of his chest.

He took a few deep breaths, trying to control his fear. He had to think logically, he told himself, he had to remain calm and clear-headed. But how could he remain calm when he knew that all the members of his personal bodyguard were in a drugged sleep? How, when there were thugs and assassins out to kill him?

There was a movement behind him and he turned. For a second his heart leapt as he thought it was Hatshepsut, the strange old nurse who had befriended him recently, soothing away the headaches which he had been having more and more frequently; and then he cursed as he saw that it was merely a trick of the light, a phantasm of his own fevered imaginings.

Ghosts! Nothing but ghosts! the boy-king cursed to himself. Ghosts, as fleeting as the strangers' faces he kept seeing in his dreams, and as distant as the voices he seemed to hear in his head when no one was talking.

With a final look behind him, he started to run again, his sandalled feet making no sound on the hard, sun-baked ground. He was heading for a small building at the far end of the gardens, which he knew led to a series of secret passages where he would be safe, when a large muscular arm shot out of a bush and grabbed him around the neck. The young Pharaoh tried to struggle, but the Nubian slave was much too strong for him, and he was dragged, kicking and cursing, out into the centre of the garden.

A man was waiting for him there, a tall, imperious man, dressed in splendid crimson robes, filigreed with streaks of silver and gold. Adamantine, blue eyes gazed at the young king down a hawk-like nose; and full and sensous lips curled upwards in an amused snarl which sent shivers of terror down the Pharaoh's spine. Although the newcomer must have been over sixty, there was an enormous strength in his wiry frame, and the young Pharaoh was instantly reminded of a cobra preparing to strike.

'Welcome.' The newcomer's voice was low and sonorous, oozing with menace.

'What do you want with me?' the young Pharaoh asked. He glanced up momentarily at the sky: the sun was low on the western horizon. 'Tell your lackey to unhand me! How dare you treat one such as I in this shoddy and treacherous manner? I am Pharaoh of all Egypt, direct descendant of the sun-god Ra!'

The older man chuckled, clearly unimpressed by the young man's indignant outburst. 'You have meddled in my affairs once too often,' he stated simply.

'Then what I have done has been for the good of all mankind,' the young man said definiatly. 'Evil such as yours should never be allowed to hold dominion in the world. And I shall fight that evil for so long as breath still remains in my body.'

The older man smirked, and the boy-king knew that he had gone too far. 'If that is your wish, O great Pharaoh, then so be it,' he chuckled.

He opened the folds of his crimson robe, and the younger man saw that, at his feet there lay a white cat. It raised itself to its haunches, and hissed at him, fixing him with baleful eyes, which, even as the boy-king watched, turned brilliantly yellow, blazing with the fire of a thousand suns.

Bolts of flame shot out of the creature's eyes, scorching the ground directly before the Pharaoh's feet. His eyes widened even further: this was no normal animal, he realised, this was a creature of the very devil himself! The cat was playing with him, he realised, teasing him as though he were a cornered mouse.

The cat hissed again, and prepared to 'fire' at him once more. The Nubian slave who was holding the Pharaoh, started to tremble. It suddenly became clear to him that if the cat were to kill his captive then he, too, would die in the conflagration. His grip on his charge faltered, and the boy-king took advantage of this to wrench himself out of his captor's grip. He raced across the garden, the Nubian and the cat in hot pursuit.

'Seize him! Destroy him!' the old man shouted. 'He must not be allowed to escape! My plans must not be thwarted! He must not be allowed to alert his own kind!'

Even as he was running, the Pharaoh heard the man's words and frowned. *Alert his own kind?* What did he mean?

Adrenaline coursed through his body, charging the synapses of his brain, and, for one brief half-instant, everything suddenly became clear for the young king. He had to call out for help, but not to his sleeping and drugged bodyguards, nor to the gods, not even to his old nurse.

There was only one place the boy-king of all Egypt could find help now: he had to call out and reach out for tomorrow . . .

Chapter Two

Tomorrow

A storm was raging over Central London, a proper zinger, thought Rog Bizley, the sort you only ever got in the tropics or the old Hammer Horror movies on late-night telly. The ones where you're alone in an old house, and you know someone – something – is watching you, but when you turn around there's no one there. And then just when you think you're safe, the vampire leaps down at you from the sky, or ghost-like arms come out of the floor to drag you screaming down to hell.

Yeah, Hammer Horror Movies, Rog thought, that's exactly what tonight is like. There was something unnatural about the forks of blue-white lightning which flashed around the old museum building, something uncanny about the way the wind howled through the yew trees outside, and the sheets of rain which hammered against the mullioned windows, like a million little devils trying to break in. The weather tonight just doesn't feel right, Rog decided.

Or, of course, the weathercaster on the TV news, could have got it wrong again. He wondered why no one ever complained to her bosses; still when you had a figure like hers he supposed she'd seldom receive any complaints.

There was a particularly loud crack of thunder, and Rog almost jumped out of his skin. He looked around nervously, as if expecting someone to be in the room with him, and then chided himself for his jumpiness. There was no way anyone could break into the museum at night, not with all this state-of-the-art security equipment: lasers, pressure points, temperature controls, and half a dozen gizmos that Rog knew he'd never be able to understand.

Rog Bizley was a night-time security guard at the James Institute, one of the country's top museums. Originally he'd been a bouncer at one of the sleazier clubs in the West End, and when he'd got this job, with its smart new uniform, walkie-talkie, and great perks, he really thought he'd gone up in the world. But there were nights like tonight when Rog really wished he was back at the club, dealing with the drunks, and eyeing up the pretty girls. At least there you could have a little bit of a laugh, and maybe have some half-decent conversation; all he had for company at the James Institute were a bunch of mouldering old dead men.

Rog swept his torch around the room. At the far end, in a glass case, were two Egyptian mummies, surrounded by artefacts that had been discovered with them in their tombs. On the wall was a large plaque with written details of the area of Egypt in which they had been found.

Rog had never bothered to read it: as far as he was concerned, the dead were dead and should be allowed to stay that way. There was something immoral about exhuming the corpses of people who had died thousands of years ago, and shipping them all the way back to England. Grave-robbing, he called it; not that he'd ever like to tell Amanda James that. She was the director of the institute, and a real weird one too: as sexy as they come, but frosty with it. If she'd let herself relax a bit she could even enjoy herself; but all she seemed to be concerned about were her precious mummies.

At the far end of the room a heavy oak door was ajar, and Rog frowned. He could have sworn the last time he made his rounds that door had been locked shut. Silently he crossed over to the door and opened it. He shone his flashlight into the room beyond.

This was the relics room where all the sacred objects that had been left in the tombs of the Pharaohs in ancient Egypt were displayed. They were supposed to accompany the dead King on his journey into the other world, Rog recalled. As far as he was concerned they were nothing but a bunch of superstitious mumbo-jumbo. At the far end of the room, mounted on the walls, was a golden and elaborate Pharaonic mask; the lapus lazuli ornamentation on it shone peculiarly in the lightning that flashed through the window. Rog had the strangest feeling that it was looking at him.

Satisfied that the room was empty, and that he must have missed the open door on his earlier round, Rog shrugged and left the relic room. As soon as he had closed the door, two figures stepped out from behind the open drapes. Had anyone been there to watch, it would have been difficult to tell whether the two newcomers had been hiding there all along, or if they had just appeared, slipping out of the inky blackness like ghosts. Certainly, it would have been impossible to say how they had entered the museum: not a window had been broken, not a alarm had been triggered.

The smaller of the two men was tubby and seemed to be in his early fifties. He would have had the reassuring appearance of someone's kindly uncle, were it not for the dangerous gleam in his saturnine eyes, and the elaborate scarlet robes he wore around his portly frame.

There was nothing of kindness about his companion. Tall and gaunt, with a tiny goatee beard, the twenty-something was dressed all in black, and his cruelly handsome face carried with it a sense of menace: this was a man who would happily pull the wings off flies for fun. He pointed a black-gloved finger to a display case in the very centre of the room.

'That's it, Mister Tate,' he whispered, and cast a wary eye at the closed door, as though expecting a security guard to come through it.

Tate nodded, a look of eager excitement on his face. 'I know, Scully,' he said. 'I remember . . .' He instructed Scully to guard the door and then approached the glass cabinet.

Displayed inside the case was a dark, purple rock, about the size of a pineapple. In the glare of a lightning-flash it shone with an eerie radiance, and the streaks of silver which ran through it seemed to sparkle like stars.

There was a small caption to one side of the stone, and Tate read:

The Marhaba Stone.
Discovered Pyramid of Sab'ba, 1995.

He smiled. At last, the stone that had been lost for so long was finally within his grasp! He cast a further cursory glance over the display case: it was made of a specially reinforced glass, and Tate knew that, even with a laser cutter, he would have trouble breaking into it. Not that that worried him, of course; Tate had access to powers, the existence of which this poor pathetic century could not even suspect. Closing his eyes, he raised his two arms to heaven, and began his incantation.

Over by the door, Scully looked curiously at Tate.

The words he was muttering were unintelligible, but for some reason Scully felt a shiver creep up his spine. The thunder was louder now, a counterpoint to Tate's words, and the lightning cast macabre shadows over his face.

Tate's voice was louder now, and Scully was worried that he would attract the attentions of one of the security guards. He urged his companion to be quieter but Tate didn't seem to hear: his face was transfixed in ecstasy.

And then there was another sound, much fainter. It was a boy's voice, scared and frightened, repeating one word over and over again:

Marhaba . . . Marhaba . . . Marhaba . . .

Scully looked at the Marhaba Stone in its glass case, and his eyes opened wide in wonder. It was glowing now, pulsating with a light so bright that he was forced to shield his eyes from the glare.

The thunder was almost deafening, and Tate had to shout to be heard above it. He raised his arms even higher, as if summoning to his aid the unchecked energies of the stars themselves. Tiny cracks started to appear in the half-inch-thick glass of the display case. The Marhaba Stone glowed even more brightly.

Marhaba . . . Marhaba . . . Marhaba . . .

Outside the lightning cracked and forked, as though delighting in the psychic and elemental forces Tate was calling into being.

And then there was an enormous explosion as the

Marhaba display case shattered, sending thousands of tiny shards of glass across the room. Tate let out a roar of triumph, and he lowered his arms to reach out greedily for the Stone, which glowed with a white-hot brilliance.

The door burst open, and Rog, attracted by the noise of the explosion burst into the relics room. He saw Tate standing by the destroyed cabinet, holding the Marhaba Stone, and laughing maniacally. And then everything went black, as Scully raised a fist and knocked him out cold.

When the other security guards found Rog a few minutes later, there was no sign of Tate or Scully. In fact, were it not for the missing Marhaba Stone and the shattered display cabinet there was no evidence of them ever having been there. No windows had been broken, no alarms had been tripped, and when they later viewed a video of the relic room they found that the tape had been mysteriously erased. It seemed that Tate and Scully had simply vanished into thin air.

As they carried the unconscious Rog out of the relic room to the waiting ambulance, one of the guards stopped for a second and frowned. He could swear he could hear something, he told his colleagues. Something really weird, like a boy's voice repeating the same word: *Marhaba . . . Marhaba . . . Marhaba . . .*

When his mates told him they couldn't hear anything, he shrugged and decided that it must have been his imagination. Of course he couldn't have heard anything, he reasoned.

But the words weren't meant for him. Three other people heard those words, and shuddered . . .

Chapter Three

Marhaba . . . Marhaba . . . Marhaba . . .

Across the vast abyss of time, the boy's words reached three young people – Adam, Ami and Megabyte. Seemingly three average teenagers, they were, in fact, *homo superius*, the Tomorrow People, the next stage in the natural course of human evolution.

Possessed of great psychic powers, and able to teleport to any spot on the globe in an instant, they were forced to keep their existence a secret from the 'saps', the *homo sapiens* who formed the rest of humanity. When not living with their families they spent most of their time in a strange spaceship, half buried in the sands of a deserted tropical island. They had no idea who had sent the spacecraft to Earth in the first place, didn't know whether they were alien beings, or perhaps even other Tomorrow people. All they did know was that the ship offered them a place of sanctuary from a world which, if it knew of their existence would only seek to exploit them.

Adam ran his fingers through his fair hair, and

looked at the central core of the ship, as if that might give him some clue. He had always regarded this large column as the heart of the ship, and within its opacity streaks of silver and gold pulsed and shone, like the nerve-channels in a human brain. Adam had often believed that the ship could think, and had wished they could find some way of communicating with it; perhaps that way they could find out who had sent it to Earth in the first place. He turned back to Ami and Megabyte.

'Someone's trying to get in touch with us,' he decided. His accent betrayed his Australian origins, although these days he spent most of the time living in the ship, rather than with his parents back home in Oz.

'A Tomorrow Person?' Ami asked. She was a pretty black girl, the same age as Adam, with long braided hair.

Adam nodded. All three of them knew that there were other TPs somewhere in the world, children and teenagers who didn't quite fit in and who were still coming to terms with the psychic abilities which would take the human race into the twenty-first century and beyond. He'd even done research in the public library, looking up reports of mysterious events throughout the world. There had been lots of such reports way back in the early seventies: if there had been Tomorrow People alive then they would have been in their late forties by now. But whenever he had tried to track down a promising lead, he had been faced with a blank.

'I think so too,' Ami said. 'But the voice is so distant . . .'

'Then it's one of two things,' Megabyte decided. He was a cheeky-faced, wise-cracking American, with a mop of copper-coloured hair. 'Whoever this guy is he's either like a million miles away . . .'

'An alien?' Ami asked.

Adam shrugged. 'It's possible,' he supposed, and looked back at the central column of the ship. Maybe its mysterious alien creators were trying to reach out across the void and communicate with them for some reason? 'Or else if he's not trying to contact us across space, then he could be calling to us across time.'

A thrill ran down Ami's spine as she instinctively realised that Adam was right. 'Could it really be a call from the future?' she asked.

'Or the past,' Adam said, 'It was like this guy was trying to give us a warning of some – ' He froze as Ami grabbed his arm excitedly and made him turn towards the centre of the ship.

There in a shimmer of green, fading in and out of existence like some dying candle, stood – *no*, Ami corrected herself, *hovered several feet above the floor* – the figure of a young man, dressed in the regalia of an ancient Egyptian Pharaoh. He seemed to see the Tomorrow People, or was at least aware of their psychic presence, and gesticulated wildly in their direction. He was clearly agitated, and his mouth opened and closed as if he was trying to tell them something – but no sound came from out of his lips.

'Talk up, kiddo! We can't hear you!' Megabyte urged but still the apparition was silent.

Adam stood up and approached the boy. 'We can't hear you!' he said, and closed his eyes and concentrated, trying to slip his own mind into that of the young boy's and hear the words he was trying to pronounce.

All around him the walls of the spaceship glowed with an eerie phosphoresence as though the machine itself was trying to lend its powers to those of Adam's. Ami and Megabyte concentrated too, and slowly words filtered into their consciousness, words belonging to an ancient language none of them had ever heard before.

'*Cheop! Sukaru! Cheopa ba'na husk'ha!*' the boy seemed to be saying. '*Marhaba! Marhaba! Cheopa ba'na husk'ha! Marhaba! Marhaba!*'

Megabyte opened his eyes and turned to his two companions. 'Don't look at me,' he said. 'I flunked Spanish . . .'

'We don't understand you!' Ami said, willing, and failing, to comprehend the strange words.

'*Sukaru! Cheopa ba'na husk'ha! Marhaba! Marhaba!*'

The young boy's voice was strained and full of emotion. Yet the more vigorously he tried to communicate to Adam, Ami and Megabyte, the more his image flickered out of existence. He reached out to them with arms, covered in golden bracelets, and then there was a flash of light, and he was gone. An eerie silence descended upon the ship.

Adam turned to the others. 'This is something really important,' he said. 'We've got to find out what . . .'

'And how do you suggest we do that?' Megabyte asked, ever the realist.

Adam stroked his chin. 'That guy was from ancient Egypt!' he decided.

'And how do you come to that conclusion?'

'He couldn't be from any other time or place,' Adam said.

Megabyte chuckled cynically. 'You saw *The Ten Commandments* on TV once and now that makes you some sort of expert on Ancient Egypt, right?' he sneered. 'Let's get real here, shall we? The guy might've been on his way to a costume party or something. For all you know he could be Ancient Eskimo!'

'Megabyte, shut up!' Adam snapped. 'There's a specialist Egyptology museum in London, round the corner from the British Museum. We go there first of all.'

'And then do what?' Megabyte continued. 'Say, "Hi, I'm Adam and I'm a Tomorrow Person. I was just talking to this Ancient Egyptian pal of mine and, well, his English ain't too hot and frankly my Ancient

Egyptian's even worse, so I figured maybe you could give me a translation . . .' " Megabyte looked superiorly at his good friend: when it came to being practical Adam could be a real wutz at times.

'You got any better ideas?' Adam asked, clearly becoming annoyed with Megabyte's flip comments.

Ami, who had remained quiet, now silenced her two friends. 'We have to do something, guys!' she insisted. She had a feeling, a strange hunch about all this. Normally she would have dismissed a similar feeling in others as precisely that – a hunch and nothing more. But Ami was a Tomorrow Person, a member of the species, *homo superior*, and flashes of precognisance weren't unheard of among their kind.

Ami had a hunch that the appearance of the boy-king portended nothing less than the end of the world.

Now this sure is some classy joint! Megabyte said to himself, as he, Adam and Ami entered the Egyptology museum. Even the young seen-it-all-before American was impressed by some of the exhibits on display, and not just because he was calculating how much money could be raised if any one of the priceless golden treasures were melted down. Some of these exhibits were over five thousand years old, dating from the time of the building of the first pyramids on the banks of the Nile. For an American whose home country had only just celebrated its two hundredth birthday, you couldn't help but being overawed by that sort of history.

'I came here once with my school class,' Ami said, as she examined a statue of Pharaoh Tuthmosis the Third. 'I remember being really haunted by all this and thinking, just who were all these people?'

They walked through several galleries, not quite sure what they were looking for, but vaguely hoping that they would come across some exhibit or item to give them a clue as to the identity of the young pharoah, and a meaning to his strange words.

Finally they reached the mummy room, and beyond that the relics room. The door to that had been sealed off, and a woman police constable was standing guard outside. As they approached her she shook her head. 'Sorry, this area's closed for today,' she said, and gestered to the strip of tape in front of the door which read: Crime Scene. No Unauthorised Access.

'We're looking for someone who can give us some information about Ancient Egypt,' Adam protested.

The WPC smiled weakly, obviously taking Adam and his two friends for a bunch of over-enthusiastic sixth-formers. 'You'd better ask someone at the desk,' she said helpfully.

'We did ask someone at the desk,' Megabyte said, not bothering to conceal the irritation in his voice. 'They told us to ask someone here!'

'You chose a bad time,' the WPC said, still polite

and charming, just as she had been told to be in police training school. 'Come back another day.'

Adam approached the cordoned off area, but the WPC stood in front of him. 'There's no entry here,' she said, now frosty and officious. 'Move along now!' Megabyte looked at Adam, and they linked minds.

– Something's going on here, Megabyte said. *Something majorly weird.*

Adam nodded his head, and was about to say something when there was a commotion behind them. An attractive Asiatic-looking woman, dressed in designer jacket and skirt, a whole bunch of dog-eared files underneath her arm, was marching towards them. There was an air of complete authority about her as she acknowledged the WPC with a nod of her finely-coiffed raven hair; the WPC lifted up the tape, allowing her access to the cordoned-off room.

Megabyte walked up to the WPC, an outraged look on his face. 'How come you let her in there and not us?' he demanded angrily.

The WPC sneered at the young American before her: she had never liked Americans ever since she'd been dumped by that visiting police sergeant a few months ago; she especially hated what she thought of as snotty-nosed or overly pushy American kids – and as far as she was concerned Megabyte fell into both of those categories.

'You're not Doctor Amanda James, the person in charge of the museum, are you!' she snapped, and took her notebook out of her top pocket to wave it threateningly at Megabyte. 'Now beat it, kid!'

If there was anything Megabyte disliked more than being told what to do, it was being called a 'kid'. Nevertheless, he uncharacteristically smiled at the WPC, threw up his arms in an acknowledgement of defeat, and returned to Adam and Ami.

'Amanda James is our woman!' he told them, and followed his two friends behind the statue of Tuhmosis the Third. Glancing around quickly to make sure that no one was watching them, the three Tomorrow People concentrated – and in a half instant their bodies had disappeared in a flash of energy, to be reassembled on the other side of the closed door.

Another half-instant was all they needed to take in the scene. The group of policemen and forensic scientists searching the remaining exhibits and walls for any trace of fingerprints or any clue as to how Tate and Scully had broken into the relics room. The smashed display cabinet in the centre of the room, the splinters of glass still laying where they had fallen in the explosion. And by the shattered cabinet Amanda James helping a burly police detective with his enquiries. Adam, Ami and Megabyte sneaked behind a large display case to eavesdrop on their conversation.

The detective frowned and looked at his notes, trying to decipher his own handwriting. 'Let's see if I've got this straight,' he said. 'This thing that has gone missing was called the Marhaba Stone.'

Behind the case, Adam, Ami and Megabyte exchanged excited looks.

– *Marhaba!* Adam said. – *It's what the boy said!*

Unaware that she was being eavesdropped on, Doctor James nodded. 'It was unearthed one month ago,' she confirmed, in a weary voice which indicated that she considered the detective's questioning a complete waste of time. 'We found it in the west Egyptian desert, in the Sab'ba desert.'

The detective nodded sagely: he remembered reading an article about the discovery in his daily newspaper, sandwiched somewhere between the Page Three pin-up and the football results. 'And what is it exactly?' he asked.

'Meteoric rock.'

The detective arched an eyebrow in interest: he loved watching science-fiction movies on the telly and at least here was something of interest. 'It was a meteor?' he asked.

Doctor James nodded patiently. 'It must have travelled vast distances across the universe,' she said. 'We guess it must have hit the Earth somewhere close to 2,000 BC, about the time of the sixth and seventh dynasties. It would have been seen and welcomed by the early Egyptians as a great gift sent to them by the gods. They worshipped it and called it the Marhaba Stone.'

The detective frowned, still little the wiser, and Doctor James continued.

'*Marhaba* means welcome,' she explained. 'Then they took the stone away and hid it behind a secret door deep inside the Sab'ba Pyramid.'

'And why should they do that?' the detective asked, and Doctor James frowned.

'I really don't know – it was a long time ago, you know!' she said bitterly, hating to admit that there was something she didn't know about the priceless Marhaba Stone. 'But I'm sure it would have had some ritualistic significance.'

'But it is just a lump of rock, isn't it, Doctor James?' the PC asked. 'What use is it to anybody? Why was it stolen?'

'I have no idea,' Doctor James said finally, and took her leave of the police officer, telling him that she was going to her office. As soon as she had left the room, Adam, Ami and Megabyte exchanged a look.

– *Let's see what else she knows!* Adam thought, and in the winking of the eye the Tomorrow People vanished from the relics room, and into the room in the direction of which Amanda James was heading.

Amanda James' office was a strange mixture of the ancient and the ultra-modern. Dotted around the office were several on-line computers, in between which the Egyptologist had placed ancient Egyptian artifacts – some genuine and immeasurably priceless, and some cheap and tacky, souvenirs she had picked up on her visits to Cairo – a miniature sphinx, for instance, or a model of the Great Pyramid of Cheops.

Every available inch of wall space was covered by huge scholarly charts, detailing all the known history of ancient Egypt, together with reproductions of the hieroglyphic symbols found on the walls of tombs. A pile of dog-eared files filled the bottom shelf of a creaking bookcase which ran the length of one wall. On top of the files had been scattered a selection of floppy disks. The entire room reeked of enormous learning, and academic dedication.

The three Tomorrow People materialised within the office and started to rifle through Amanda James' files for any mention of the Marhaba Stone. But the scientist's files were filled with hieroglyphical writings which, as far as Adam, Ami and Megabyte were concerned, were little more than ancient gobblydegook, and detailed references to learned theses and journals.

It seemed they had lucked out until Megabyte pointed to a large blown-up photograph on the wall: the Marhaba Stone itself. It was breathtaking, even when reproduced in black-and-white, and somehow they all intuited that here was no ordinary meteor that had fallen out of the sky: here was an object of terrific importance and almost limitless power. So entranced were the three of them by the photo that none of them heard the door to the office click open, or saw Amanda James stride resolutely into the middle of the room.

'These are private offices,' she said, trying to muster as much justified outrage as she could at finding three meddlesome teenagers in her private quarters. 'You can't just come in here.'

'We need some answers,' Ami said and nodded over to the photo on the wall. 'Answers to do with the Marhaba Stone.'

'What do you know about that,' Amanda asked warily, careful not to give too much away.

'We know it's been stolen,' Ami continued and almost instantly realised her mistake: the press had not yet received news of the robbery, so how could they have known of the Stone's disappearance – unless they had something to do with its theft?

Amanda James glanced involuntarily at the office door, and wondered whether she ought to call in the police inspector stationed outside. Instead she turned uncertainly on the three intruders.

'How do you know it's been stolen?' she demanded suspiciously. 'Just who are you?'

Adam strode forwards, closed his eyes, and repeated the words the boy-king had spoken to them. '*Sukaru . . . Ba'na husk'ha . . . Marhaba . . .*' He opened his eyes again, and Amanda was struck by their unearthly brilliance as they stared questioningly at her. 'Those are ancient Egyptian words,' he said. 'What do they mean.'

Amanda James stepped back and held on to her desk for support: she was visibly shaken. 'Is this a joke?' she asked, and there was an uncertain tremor in her voice which few people had ever heard before. 'Ancient Egyptian is a dead language that hasn't been spoken in thousands of years. Nobody knows what it sounded like.'

Adam walked over to the bookshelf and picked up a small-scale reproduction of one of the obelisks from the archaeological site at Karnak on the banks of the River Nile; he ran his long fingers over the hieroglyphs on its side. 'But it is written down,' he said.

'That's right. But what has this got to do with the Marhaba Stone.

Megabyte shrugged. 'We're not sure,' he admitted. 'Maybe nothing. Maybe something.'

Adam closed his eyes again. '*Cheopa . . . Cheopa . . .*' he intoned. '*Ba'na husk'ha . . .*'

'*Cheopa!*' Amanda said, and her lips were trembling, as she heard the ancient words on the lips of a boy who couldn't be much more than eighteen. 'Who told you that word?'

'You know what it means?' Adam asked.

'I heard that word once before,' she told him. 'I was on a dig in Egypt near Cairo, and I met a man there who claimed he was a hundred and twenty-nine years old – ' she continued, ignoring the TPs' incredulous looks – 'He spoke in a weird mixture of modern Egyptian Arabic and a strange local dialect.'

Amanda regarded Adam, Ami and Megabyte for a moment, wondering whether to trust them or not. Finally she decided, and marched smartly over to where Adam was standing by the bookcase. She ran her forefinger along a shelf loaded down with ancient-looking leather-bound books, all of which, Adam could see, were on the subject of the hieroglyphs of Ancient Egypt. Finally she lighted on the one she wanted; a tattered paperback diary.

She took it from the shelf and Adam and the others followed her to the desk where she opened the scruffy volume. The pages were full of individual hieroglyphics, each of them painstakingly written in by Doctor James herself. Listed alongside each hieroglyphic was its equivalent form in modern Egyptian Arabic, as well as a phonetic transliteration of the word into modern English: it was, to all intents and purposes, a hieroglyphic-English dictionary.

'Is it possible that some of those ancient words have survived down the centuries?' Ami wondered out aloud, as Amanda turned the pages of the book, searching for one particular word, oblivious, in all her excitement, to everything else.

'*Marhaba* still gets used,' Adam said, and pored over the dictionary together with Ami and Megabyte. 'There must be others as well . . .'

'That's what I thought,' Amanda said. 'That's why I wrote them down.' She gave a small whoop of triumph and her finger pointed to one particular word. 'There it is!'

Adam bent down to examine the hieroglyph more closely. Alongside it was written its Arabic equivalent – *Cheopa* – and next to that its modern-day English version.

'*Cheopa* means Cleopatra!' Adam realised, and beside him Adam nodded her head enthusiastically.

'That's right!' she said. '*Cheopa* is the ancient form of the name Cleopatra.'

Megabyte, who had not only flunked Spanish but ancient history as well, decided that he needed to ask for clarification. 'Hey, you mean Cleopatra, the Queen of Egypt.'

Adam shot him a withering look. 'No, Megabyte, Cleopatra, the glove puppet,' he said sarcastically. He turned back to Doctor James, and asked her to look up the word *ba'na*. Caught up in Adam's enthusiasm, she flicked back through the dictionary.

'There it is!' Adam cried. '*Ba'na* means "sacred"!'

Ami exchanged blank looks with him and Megabyte: '"Cleopatra the Sacred"?'

Amanda shook her head. 'No, the sentence structure works the other way round, in Ancient Egyptian,' she said. '*Cheopa ba'na husk-ha* means "the sacred something of Cleopatra"!'

Adam took the book from Amanda's hands and

turned the pages to the h's, where he jabbed a finger at the entry. '*Hush-ha* means "obelisk"!' he said, a note of triumph in his voice.

'Then *cheopa ba'na hush'ha* means "the sacred obelisk of Cleopatra"!' Amanda announced.

Megabyte decided that he wasn't going to be excluded from the conversation any longer: 'Look, guys, call me Walnut Brain if you like but am I the only person here who doesn't understand a single word of all this?'

Doctor James closed her dictionary and looked up at Megabyte. 'The ancient Egyptians used to build these huge squared pillars made of solid stone,' she explained to him. 'They called them obelisks.'

'So what?' Megabyte said, unimpressed.

'Don't you see, Megabyte?' Adam said, quickly losing patience with his friend's slow-wittedness. 'It's fantastic: the sacred obelisk of Cleopatra that that boy was telling us about is Cleopatra's Needle!'

Megabyte sighed. 'Sure, it's great, sure it's fantastic! Someone catch me before I faint,' he gibed. 'And what the heck is Cleopatra's Needle when it's at home?'

Chapter Four

As far as Megabyte was concerned, a lump of old stone was a lump of old stone was a lump of old stone, and neither Adam nor Ami could convince him otherwise, as they stared up in wonder at the granite majesty of the ancient monument, perched on the north bank of the River Thames.

It towered twenty-one metres high, surmounted by a small pyramid pointing to the heavens, and around its base black Sphinx statues stood guard, as though offering it protection from the hordes of tourists who swarmed around it. Even the elaborate hieroglyphics carved deep into its grey surface failed to impress him: he'd seen fancier designs on the latest CD cover from Bon Jovi.

'This is it?' he scoffed, but Ami chose to ignore him.

'It's beautiful,' she said: there was something awe-inspiring about the obelisk, she felt. Cleopatra's Needle was over seventeen centuries old, so the London Tourist Board plaque at the base of the obelisk told her. The men who had quarried the stone and constructed it were long since dead, turned to dust in the boundless sands of Egypt; and yet it was here, a direct link to that past time, to a time of magic and wonder. It was somehow comforting to think that it had survived the centuries to be brought here to London.

'Look, you guys, you said Egypt,' Megabyte pointed out. He gestured towards the eastern horizon at the familiar London skyline: Saint Paul's Cathedral, the Lloyds Building, and far off in the distance the new office tower which peculiarly enough resembled the shape of the Needle itself, right down to the glass and steel pyramid which crowned its summit, and blazed red and gold in the late morning sun. 'It may have escaped your notice but this is London, England. What's it doing here?'

'How should I know, Megabyte?' Adam grumbled. 'Maybe it's taking a holiday!'

Ami moved even closer to the Needle, and her face broke into a grin. 'I know,' she said. 'We learnt about it in our history lessons at school. It was originally built round the fifteenth century BC, by Pharaoh called Tuthmosis the Third.'

'You mean the guy whose statue we saw in the museum?' Adam asked.

'That's right,' Ami said. 'And it was moved from Egypt and brought here to London towards the end of the last century.'

'So how does Cleopatra fit into all this?' Adam was confused. 'If I remember my history right she lived around two thousand years ago – and not seventeen centuries ago like your Tuthmosis.'

'That was just a name that the Press gave to the obelisk,' Ami said. 'It's really got nothing to do with Cleopatra at all!'

Megabyte groaned. 'Which means that we're precisely back where we started!' Adam flashed him a look which warned him to shut up.

Ami was standing directly in front of the obelisk now and she reached out a hand to touch it. Her fingers tingled as she stroked its cold surface, and for a second Ami could almost feel the sun of Ancient Egypt on the back of her hand, and taste the tang of the desert winds on her tongue. She was grinning now from ear to ear, her entire body suffused with an indescribable feeling of well-being. She moved around the base of the monument, and walked into the shadow of the Needle.

Suddenly she felt incredibly cold and her smile vanished from her face. She looked up at the Needle, and her whole soul was filled with a sense of dread. Once again, she knew that she was looking at the end of the world. She staggered back from the monument and would have fainted, had Adam not ran to her side, and stopped her falling.

'Ami? Are you OK?' he asked, but before she could answer there was a commotion behind them, on the stone steps leading to the Needle. They all turned to see what was causing the disturbance.

'Look out, guys,' Megabyte sighed. 'It's psycho's day out!'

Bounding down the steps towards them was an elderly woman, dressed in a peculiar assortment of raggedy and cast-off clothes, most of which had obviously seen better days. The wisp of silvery white hair which peeked out from under her headscarf suggested a woman of about sixty years old, although her face was remarkably free from lines, and there was a startling quality and a ready intelligence in her eyes which recalled those of a much younger woman. She was carrying a hand-made placard, on which had been scrawled the words *Take me home!* As she approached Adam, Ami, Megabyte and several groups of tourists moved out of her way.

'"Take me home!" she wails and weeps, and weeps and wails!' the woman declaimed, in a voice so passionate that her several chins wobbled when she spoke. "Won't anybody take me home!"'

She had apparently not noticed the Tomorrow People yet, and she was addressing a group of Japanese tourists, who could scarcely believe their luck in having just stumbled across a real-life genuine example of the quintessential British eccentric. The sound of clicking Nikons threatened to drown out the woman's voice.

'More than a hundred and twenty years she's languished here!' she cried, and indicated Cleopatra's

Needle with a grand flourish of her hand. 'Forsaken! A stranger in a strange and unfriendly land!'

The Japanese tourists clapped delightedly, and chattered to each other in their own language, clearly not understanding a word of what the old woman was saying. When they had finished taking their photographs, they bowed graciously to the old woman and left. By the base of Cleopatra's Needle Adam, Ami and Megabyte each stifled a giggle.

Forlorn and forsaken, the old woman started to walk disconsolately to the Needle, all the time muttering strange unintelligible words to herself. Her head was bowed in disappointment and she trudged along like a weary foot soldier going off to battle.

Then she saw Adam, Ami and Megabyte, and her face lit up. An enormous grin came over her face and her eyes misted with emotion, as if she was seeing for the first time in an eternity three dearly beloved old friends. She dropped her placard on to the ground, and raised her hands to her mouth in an expression of delight and disbelief. *Is it really you?* her eyes seemed to be saying.

Slowly she started walking towards them. Megabyte started whistling self-consciously to himself: back home in the States the weirdoes always seemed to get a fix on him, and now it looked as if their UK cousins were doing the same.

Ami, on the other hand, smiled: there was something innately trustworthy about this odd, little, old lady, she knew, and the expression of delight on her face was nothing short of angelic.

The woman stopped a few paces away from them, and wiped a tear from her eye. 'You've come!' she said, in a voice choked with emotion. 'You've really come at long last! I've waited such a long, long time!' She reached out her hand and gave each of them a hearty handshake.

Ami smiled at the old lady. 'Do we know you?' she asked.

'You will know me,' she promised, and looked briefly over her shoulder to make sure that no one was watching or eavesdropping on them. 'We've a lot to do together, and very little time in which to do it!'

Megabyte looked over at Adam as if to say *What a nutter*, but Adam seemed to be as much taken in by the weird, old lady as Ami.

The old woman gestured towards Cleopatra's Needle. 'The sacred obelisk of Cleopatra,' she said. 'Ripped from its home in Heliopolis, toppled into the sands of Alexandria, and then plucked from her native soil by evil men who I've chased across the centuries . . .' She paused, realising from the blank expressions on the faces of Adam, Ami and Megabyte that she was running ahead of herself. She let out a self-conscious chuckle. 'Goodness me, you must think I'm completely crackers!'

'Absolutely not!' Megabyte lied, and took a small step away from the 'nutter'. He glanced at Adam. – *Let's get outta here!*

'Fret not – it will all become clear, and sooner than you think,' the old woman reassured him.

Just as if she had read his mind, Megabyte suddenly realised.

'My name is Millicent F. Rutherford,' she introduced herself and shook each of their hands in turn once again. 'And you, of course, are Ami, Megabyte and Adam.'

The three Tomorrow People exchanged incredulous looks: how could this dotty old woman know their names, when until only a few moments ago they had never even met? Before they could ask, Millicent went on.

'It's up to all of us now,' she said, and there was no mistaking the urgency in her voice. 'There's danger all around us. Nothing is what it seems. The future of the planet is in our hands now.' She looked around again, to reassure herself once again that they weren't being watched. 'He's close now, very close!' she whispered, and reached into one of her pockets and pulled out a picture postcard, which she handed over to Adam.

The front of the postcard was a sepia-toned photograph of a rambling British folly; he read the name underneath the picture: Temple Hall. It was an old house in north London, built sometime in the early nineteenth century; Adam had passed by it once and he recalled the local kids saying that it was haunted.

'Meet me here later,' she said, and in response to

Ami's question of when they should meet her, said enigmatically: 'You'll know when, Ami! I'm so glad you've come!'

And with that Millicent turned and strode quickly away from them, at a speed none of them would have thought a woman as old as her capable of.

Adam, Ami and Megabyte looked at each other: who was this crazy woman? And why had she been so concerned that someone was watching them? The place was empty – even the Japanese tourists had disappeared on to the next stage of their whirlwind London tour.

When Adam, Ami and Megabyte looked up Millicent was nowhere to be seen. She had simply vanished into thin air, and, had it not been for the postcard that Adam was clutching in his hand, there would have been no evidence that she had been there at all . . .

Adam, Ami and Megabyte were wrong: someone had indeed been watching them, had been spying on them ever since they had visited the room from which the Marhaba Stone had been stolen. He had seen them visit Cleopatra's Needle and had listened in on every detail of their conversation with Millicent Rutherford.

High above the city of London, alone in his windowless sanctuary into which no daylight came, the man some knew as Sam Rees sat waiting patiently, like a spider at the centre of its web. The only noise in the large and icy room was the sound of Sam Rees drumming his long and gnarled fingers on his desk, which had been fashioned out of purest ebony. Occasionally Sam Rees would reach out and stroke the white cat which sat on the desk, and neither mewed nor purred, just watched its master through cold, unblinking eyes.

On the desk before him was a small glass pyramid, within which Sam Rees could see the figures of Adam, Ami and Megabyte on the Embankment, wondering where Millicent might have disappeared to. A small smile crossed his full and sensuous lips and his adamantine, blue eyes blazed with triumph.

The three youngsters were fools, he decided, inferior things despite their powers of telepathy and teleportation. Sam Rees had mastered such powers many long years ago; but then Sam Rees was not of their kind, he came from a race much older and more powerful than they could ever have conceived, even in their darkest dreams.

These Tomorrow People, as they so naively called themselves, had no sense of guile or cunning, no conception of the supreme order of things: for goodness' sake, they were physically incapable of killing another human being! The inability to kill, the inability to bend others to your will, they were supreme failings as far as Sam Rees was concerned. He need have little concern for these mere youngsters.

But Millicent F. Rutherford was another matter altogether, Sam Rees concluded. He knew the woman of old, and recognised in her an effective and deadly foe. For a brief second a shadow of doubt passed over Sam Rees's brow. If she allied her talents to those of these Tomorrow People, then who knew what would happen?

Sam Rees lifted his eyes heavenwards. On the wall behind him there hung a huge stone bird, a symbol of Ancient Egypt. And clutched in the bird's claw, glowing with an unnatural light was the Marhaba Stone, bathing Sam Rees in its brilliance, like a spotlight on an actor.

The man known as Sam Rees smiled once more: with the power of the Marhaba Stone in his possession who would dare to stand against him? Sam Rees looked down once more into the glass pyramid, willing another image to appear within it. Adam, Ami and Megabyte disappeared to be replaced by a picture of the night sky, and of one group of seven stars in particular.

Soon, Sam Rees, said to himself. Soon all his plans would finally bear fruit. Soon he would possess power without measure, a power over which no man had had mastery since the dawn of time. Soon the world would be remade new, a world in his own choosing, a world in which the only will would be that of Sam Rees, in which the only thoughts would be those that Sam Rees allowed.

If Sam Rees had been a man of emotion he would have thrown his head back and laughed triumphantly. Instead he merely stared into the glass pyramid, stroked his cat, and waited.

For the man some knew as Sam Rees possessed infinite patience. He could wait thousands of years if he had to . . .

Chapter Five

'This whole thing is driving me nuts!' Megabyte complained as he teleported back to the spaceship with Ami. 'All this end-of-the-world baloney! Give me a break!'

'You're wrong, Megabyte,' Ami said, and threw herself down on one of the benches which lined the wall. It instantly readjusted itself to fit the contours of her body. 'Millicent knows things.'

'And how do you figure that one out?' Megabyte asked cynically.

'I *know*, that's all,' Ami said. To any one else it would have seemed a pretty feeble explanation; but Megabyte was a Tomorrow Person too, and he'd long ago learnt to trust his own instincts and hunches. 'But why would she give us an old postcard of this Temple Hall place?'

'Maybe it's the asylum she escaped from,' Megabyte suggested, only half-jokingly. Ami glared at him.

'We'll find out soon enough,' Ami said. 'Adam's

teleported there now. I'm sure that house fits into the whole thing somehow. The voice, that boy, those words: it can't just be a coincidence. And I'm sure we were sent to Cleopatra's Needle to meet Millicent.'

Megabyte sat down next to her. 'OK, just suppose you're right,' he said, although in his heart he knew that she was. 'What was she going on about, lugging two hundred tons of rock back to Egypt. Why? What for?'

'We'll find out,' Ami said with certainty, and then froze. She pointed over to the centre of the ship. There in a flickering of green the Egyptian boy had appeared once again. The two of them leapt to their feet and rushed over to him.

'Who are you?' Ami cried, looking the boy in the eye. She noticed that the area around his eyes were heavily made-up, lined with dark streaks of kohl.

Sukaru! the boy said, although no words came from his mouth. *Ma'hat chep sura!*

'We don't understand you, kiddo!' Megabyte said, but the boy seemed not to hear him, of if he did he made no response. He continued to gesticulate wildly, while all the time his image faded in and out of existence.

'What's your name?' Ami said, and when the boy didn't reply, she opened her mind to him – *I'm Ami. What's your name?*

The boy registered Ami's thoughts, and he relaxed

and let out an enormous sigh of relief. It was as though he were seeing Ami and Megabyte for the first time: at last he had made contact with his own kind! He pointed at himself with a heavily-bejewelled finger, and reached into their own minds.

– Tut . . . 'ank . . . Amun. Amun! Tut . . . 'ankh . . . Amun!

Ami couldn't believe what she was hearing. She turned to Megabyte. 'Tut . . . 'ankh . . . Amun! He's Tutankhamun! The boy pharaoh! The child king of Ancient Egypt!'

Stunned, Megabyte looked back at the boy, and recognised something in his eyes, a certain sharpness and understanding. Ami had that look in her eye too, as had Adam, and Kevin and Lisa, the two other TPs he knew.

'Tutankhamun was a Tomorrow Person!'

'He must have been one of the very first,' Ami said. 'Adam was right! He's talking to us across forty centuries!'

Megabyte still couldn't quite get a grip on the idea. He stared back at Tutankhamun, whose image was fading by the second. 'It's like he was right here with us, in the same place but in a different time!'

Tutankhamun reached into their minds again, and this time his tone was much more agitated. – *Amtoudi!* he said. – *Amtoudi! Sujaru, ma'hat chep sura! Amtoudi! Amtoudi! Amtoudi* . . . His voice was becoming fainter and fainter.

'I don't know how long we can hold him!' Ami said. The spaceship's central core hummed, and pulsed with light, trying to stabilise the image of the boy-king.

– *What are you trying to warn us against?* Ami asked him. – *What are you trying to say?*

Tutankhamun pointed up towards the roof of the ship. – *Amtoudi! Amtoudi! Amtou . . .*

'We're losing him!' Megabyte said. Tutankhamun was now little more than a blur of green in the centre of the ship.

'Focus!' Ami cried, and joined her mind with Megabyte's. 'Concentrate!'

Slowly Tutankhamun came back into focus – *Sukaru Amtoudi!* he wailed – *Amtoudi! Amtoudi! Amtoudi!*

And then there was a flash of light and the image of Tutankhamun vanished. Exhausted, Ami and Megabyte fell back on to the benches.

'Amtoudi?' Ami said, struggling to catch her breath. 'What is Amtoudi?'

Temple Hall wouldn't have looked out of place in an *Addams Family* movie, Adam decided as he strolled up the gravel driveway which led to the house. It was a run-down Gothic pile, all towers and gargoyles, and set in its own over-grown grounds on the edge of London's Highgate Cemetery. Approaching it in the afternoon gave him the major creeps; he hardly dared think what it would be like at night.

Adam sneaked up to a side window, and peered into the house. Apart from a few items of tatty furniture, and some threadbare wall hangings, the place seemed as empty and as dead as a grave. Adam gulped. He'd prefer not to think about things like that.

He jumped as the huge oaken front door creaked open in true Hammer horror movie style, and a gaunt face peered out at him, looking Adam up and down with dark eyes, like a King Cobra considering its lunch. Adam stepped back and gulped: this guy was seriously weird, he thought, the sort of creep who could give even Bela Lugosi a good run for his money.

'Er, hi . . .' Adam said, when Scully didn't speak. 'I didn't know anyone was living here . . .'

'This is a private residence,' Scully said. 'Mister Tate does not welcome visitors.'

'Mister Tate? Could I have a word with him, please?'

'Mister Tate is out of the country,' was Scully's reply.

'D'you know when he'll be back?'

Scully smiled – no, Adam decided, leered. 'That all depends on when he leaves . . .' He slammed the door in Adam's face.

Yeah, well thanks for nothing, Adam thought and

moved away from the door. As he did so he had the feeling that he was being watched, and indeed Scully had now joined Tate by a high window to look down on their unwelcome visitor. Rather than turn around, Adam jammed his hands into the pockets of his Levi's and sauntered off down the path. When he knew he was out of sight of Tate and Scully, he closed his eyes, and concentrated.

– Megabyte? I think I'm on to something here! I need your help!

Back in the spaceship Megabyte responded to Adam's call. By his side Ami was writing down on a notepad as many of Tutankhamun's words as she could recall.

– *I'm on my way, Adam*, he said, and turned to Ami. 'You coming?'

Ami shook her head. 'I've got to go and see Millicent,' she said. 'She told us that we'd know when it was time to meet her again.' There was a mysterious look in Ami's eyes. 'It's time.'

Megabyte nodded. He wasn't sure what sort of psychic bond had developed between Ami and Millicent – maybe Ami didn't know herself – but he had learnt to trust her instincts. Nodding a brief farewell, he teleported out of the ship.

'So what do you want me to do, old buddy?' Megabyte said, as soon as he had joined Adam in the grounds of Temple Hall. Adam pointed over to the building.

'I need to see inside that house,' he explained.

'So teleport in,' Megabyte said.

'I can't risk being caught,' Adam said. 'We need to create a diversion.'

Megabyte's face lit up, and he made a show of dusting his hands, ready for action. 'Hey, diversions are my speciality!'

Adam slapped him on the shoulder. 'I knew I could count on you!' he grinned, and watched Megabyte walk up the path to the house.

This time the door was creaked open by both Tate and Scully. Scully was dressed in his usual black suit, but Tate was wearing a long scarlet robe, covered with ornate and esoteric symbols. There was something about the shorter man which unnerved Megabyte; as Tate peered down into Megabyte's eyes, it seemed as if he was trying to read his thoughts.

And that's impossible, isn't it? Megabyte told himself. *After all, he's just some fat guy who gets a weird kick out of dressing up like an extra from The Rocky Horror Show. It's not like he's a telepath . . .*

'Hi, I'm lost,' he began in his best dumb American tourist voice. 'I'm looking for the South Circular – am I close?'

Scully smiled, and took one step out of the doorway; Megabyte's smile faded, and he took two steps back.

'I'm afraid you have made a . . . mistake,' Tate said, the tone in his voice indicating that he didn't believe Megabyte's story in the slightest. 'You shouldn't have come this way – you're travelling in entirely the wrong direction.'

'I guess it's easy to lose your way on these minor roads,' Megabyte bumbled.

'Maybe next time you will plan your journey more carefully,' Tate suggested slyly.

Scully sniggered, and placed a black-gloved hand on Megabyte's shoulder: the hand was cold to the touch. 'Come inside,' Scully oozed. 'We have a road map somewhere – we may be able to sort you out . . .'

Megabyte gulped as he recognised the dangerous glint in the man's dark, unfathomable eyes: he was in deep trouble now.

As soon as Tate and Scully had answered the door to Megabyte, Adam had teleported into the house. The room he found himself in was large but sparsely furnished. A few items were dotted around the place to give it the impression of being lived in; but their delapidated state, and the threadbare curtains, showed that no one had actually made Temple Hall their home in a long time.

Several paintings hung on one wall – cheap reproductions of old masters, Adam guessed, their paintwork old and faded. One painting described a stylised encounter between Cleopatra, Queen of the Nile, and the Roman emperor Augustus; it was painted in the Victorian style, but even Adam could tell that it had probably been picked up in a junk stall within the past ten years.

However, hanging on the opposite wall, and dominating the entire room was a golden Egyptian death mask, which reminded Adam of the one they had seen in Doctor James' museum.

He moved across the room to inspect it more closely – was it his imagination, or did it seem to be glowing faintly with its own light? The blank eyes, the colour of lapis lazuli, somehow seemed to be watching him – but that was stupid, wasn't it? After all, it was only a mask . . . He reached out a hand to touch it, and then stopped: there was something evil about this mask, he instinctively realised.

Outside in the hallway he could hear Tate and Scully talking to Megabyte. From the sound of it Megabyte's diversion wouldn't be lasting much longer. Adam looked around at the rest of the room. In the centre stood a large table, about the size of a family dining table. A large silken dust sheet covered the table, concealing something beneath: Adam moved over and swiped off the sheet.

On the table top was an architectural model of a vast city, made out of white-painted wood, and complete with towering buildings, massive temples, and broad interconnecting highways. The city was heptagonal in shape, and at each of the seven points there stood a huge obelisk: Adam was instantly reminded of Cleopatra's Needle on the Embankment.

The whole model ressembled some modern-day architect's vision of an Ancient Egyptian city but re-defined for the twenty-first century. At the centre of the model a huge pyramid dominated the city, and it was on this pyramid that all the highways converged. A strange symbol had been painted on to each of the pyramid's four sides, a symbol which Adam recognised from the photograph he'd seen in Doctor James' office: it was a graphic representation of the Marhaba Stone. He was about to investigate further, when he heard Megabyte calling out to him.

– *Adam! Get out of here! Now!*

As Adam picked up the white sheet that had been covering the model city, he accidentally knocked one of the wooden buildings over. Several wooden blocks fell clattering to the floor. Adam cursed and hurriedly picked up the blocks of wood: in the hallway outside he could hear Megabyte bidding a hasty goodbye to Tate and Scully, and the two men banging the heavy oaken door shut.

Cursing to himself, Adam frantically tried to re-arrange the pieces back together again; there were only seconds left before Tate and Scully would return. The handle to the door was turning as he replaced the final piece and swooped the silk dust sheet back over the table.

'We should have killed him,' Scully said, and cracked his knuckles.

'Possibly,' Tate said thoughtfully, and then frowned. He looked around the room: it was empty but a faint electrical charge still hung in the air, the result of Adam's teleporting away to safety. 'First the Australian boy and now him . . .'

'We should have killed him,' Scully repeated.

'The last thing we need at this stage is any kind of undue attention to ourselves,' Tate reminded him, even though Scully promised him that he was an expert at getting rid of unwanted corpses. 'Now, come! We have a task to perform! Is the transport prepared?'

'Of course, Mister Tate,' Scully confirmed and followed his master out of the room. 'We still should have killed him,' he grumbled. Scully hadn't killed anyone for several weeks now: if this kept up then he was going to lose his touch.

Ami knew where to find Millicent. About an hour after Adam and Megabyte had teleported away from Temple Hall, she and the old lady were sitting on the Embankment wall, by Cleopatra's Needle, staring thoughtfully into the Thames. By Millicent's side was the early edition of the *Evening Standard*. Tucked away on page seven there was a small one-column report of the break-in at the museum.

'The theft of the Marhaba Stone could be the final link in his plan,' Millicent said, not looking at Ami, but watching the muddy waters of the Thames. There was an immense sadness in her eyes.

'Who, Millicent?' Ami asked. 'Who are you talking about?'

Millicent didn't seem to hear. 'If we're to stop it, we're going to have to act very, very fast,' she said. 'He can actually do it this time!'

'I don't understand, Millicent!'

Millicent turned and grabbed Ami by the arm: her grip was powerful for such a seemingly frail old lady. 'It's exactly the prediction of the ancient priests,' she said. "The stone shall move, the stars will shine, a shadow long shall fall upon the earth . . ."'

Ami shuddered; and then she was aware that Millicent was no longer looking at her. Instead she was looking over her shoulder at an old-fashioned black limousine which was just pulling up at the kerb. Two men Ami didn't recognise – Tate and Scully – stepped out and started walking slowly towards them.

Millicent's face fell, yet she betrayed no sense of fear. Rather there was a look of acceptance on her face, as if all her life had been leading up to this one moment. Scully walked up to Millicent, ignoring Ami completely.

'Would you please come with us, Madam?' Scully said, and held out his hand to Millicent. His voice was polite, charm personified: it made Ami's blood run cold.

Millicent hung her head, calmly accepting her fate, as Scully and Tate took her by the arms, and started to lead her away.

'What do you think you're doing?' Ami demanded, and strode after them as they bundled Millicent into the waiting limo. 'You can't do this!'

Neither Tate nor Scully replied. Tate looked patronisingly at Ami as he followed Millicent into the back of the car; Scully simply sneered, and got into the driver's seat.

'Don't worry about me, Ami,' Millicent said sadly as the car started to move away. 'Look in the papers – you *must* look in the papers!'

'What papers, Millicent?' Ami asked and started to run after the car as it gathered speed and filtered into the heavy London traffic.

– Adam! Megabyte! I need you!

Adam and Megabyte responded in seconds, and appeared out of sight behind Cleopatra's Needle in a flash of energy. They ran over to Ami by the roadside.

'They're taking Millicent!' she cried and pointed after the fast-disappearing limo. There was no way they could catch up with it, and they didn't dare teleport in front of half a hundred drivers on the main road.

Adam wasted no time. There was a gang of young kids hanging around the base of the Needle; around the neck of one of them hung a pair of speed skates.

He raced over to him, and snatched the skates. Before the kid had time to react Adam had already kicked off his own sneakers and was tying up the laces of the skates. Meanwhile Ami and Megabyte were busy negotiating the sale of the skates; Megabyte sighed and took out his wallet.

His heart pounding, and every muscle in his legs aching, Adam raced after the departing limo, flashing from road to pavement, and weaving in and out of the heavy traffic. Aware that they were being followed, Scully increased his speed – 'I told you we should have killed them!' he growled as he ran a red light, and took a U-turn, heading towards the City.

Adam followed suit, narrowly avoiding an approaching lorry, and then hit a left, up a narrow street. He knew that the limo would be caught up in the heavy Embankment traffic: if he could take several short-cuts down tiny alleys and pedestrian walkways he might just be able to catch up with Millicent and her abductors.

He zoomed out of a side-street, and back on to the main road. For a horrible second he thought that he had lost the limo. Then he saw it, hurtling along Upper Thames Street, heading, so he guessed, to the East End. Summoning up his last reserves of strength he followed the car.

The chase lasted for another ten minutes, with Adam gaining a little on the car every second. Sure enough, they were heading for the East End, and, as he sped along the road and pavements, Adam recognised the Monument to the Great Fire, the Tower of London, Saint Katharine's Dock, and, in the distance, the towering new office block which dominated the horizon for miles around.

They were in the warehouse district now, and suddenly the car took a sharp left, and roared up a narrow street. Taken unawares, Adam missed the turning and screeched to a halt on his speed skates. He spun around and skated up the street; a sign on the corner read *No Exit*. The street was a cul-de-sac: there was no possible way out.

The car wasn't there.

Adam skated to a halt, a baffled look on his face, and he ran his fingers through his hair. There were several parked cars in the street, but of the limo there was no sign. It had just vanished into thin air, just as mysteriously as Millicent had on their first meeting.

And that was impossible. Wasn't it?

Shaking his head, Adam sat down on the kerb and started to untie his skates. There had to be a sensible explanation for the limo's disappearance, he reasoned. It wasn't as if Millicent's abductors could just teleport away, like he and Ami and Megabyte could. Was it?

A sudden movement made him leap to his feet, and he tensed, ready for danger. Then he smiled and relaxed, when he saw a white cat slink out from behind an overturned dustbin. Adam crouched down, and held out his hand to the cat, encouraging it to come up to him to be stroked.

The cat looked at him, and hissed.

Adam suddenly realised that this was no ordinary street cat.

This was evil incarnate.

Two bolts of eldritch-green energy blazed from the cat's eyes, striking the warehouse wall just behind Adam, which exploded in a shower of dust and debris. Wasting no time, Adam leapt to his feet, leaping over a pile of wooden crates.

The cat fired again, this time striking the crates, which burst into flames.

There was nowhere for Adam to hide, and he knew that he couldn't reach the one exit from the street in time. Desperately he looked around for anything which could protect him from the cat.

Nothing.

The cat advanced on him, stalking him like a lion would a stricken gazelle. The cat licked its lips: it was hungry and it would not stop until it and its master had feasted on Adam's very soul.

Adam prepared to teleport.

And found he couldn't. The cat was exerting some baleful influence over him, which was numbing his powers. He panicked, looking around for somewhere to hide. He ran over to one of the parked cars: if only he could get into one of them he might still be able to drive away. He tugged at the driver's door: it was locked.

There was no escape.

Adam dropped to the ground and rolled underneath the car. Frantically. Foolishly.

The cat directed its laser vision on to the car's fuel tank, and fired. The car exploded in a massive ball of flames.

For several long seconds the cat regarded the burning wreck, making sure that there was no movement. But how could there be? It reasoned to itself. How could anyone survive such a massive conflagration.

Satisfied with its handiwork, the servant of Sam Rees turned and padded away. One enemy had been destroyed; now there were only two more left.

It was only then that the cat started to purr happily to itself.

Chapter Six

The huge double doors to Sam Rees's sanctuary opened silently, but Sam Rees, sitting on a throne on a raised dais, showed no emotion as he recognised the person Tate and Scully were escorting into his private domain. Emotions were for lesser beings, Sam Rees had long since decided; even so he could not suppress a mild sense of curiosity at finally coming face-to-face with the power that had opposed him for so long.

'We have her,' Tate said triumphantly, and glanced at Millicent, who shrugged off both him and Scully. She stared at Sam Rees, recognising him for who he was; but there was no hate in her eyes. As far as Millicent was concerned, hate was for lesser creatures.

Sam Rees looked at Tate. 'There is danger,' he said, in that emotionless monotone of his which nevertheless struck terror in the hearts of all those who heard it. 'There are new enemies who seek to destroy what we shall create.'

Tate's podgy face fell in a look of disappointment.

'Who are these people, my lord?' he asked, although he knew full well to whom his master was referring.

Scully leant forward to speak in Tate's ear: 'See! I told you we should have killed them!' He lowered his voice so Sam Rees couldn't hear him, but it was to no avail: Sam Rees heard everything.

'Silence.' Sam Rees's emotionless tone brooked no opposition, and Scully froze. There was a strange unearthly quality about Sam Rees, something which Scully thought wasn't quite of this world. Rees turned his attention to Tate.

'Your expression causes me concern,' he stated.

'Fear not, my lord,' Tate said, and unsuccessfully tried to affect an air of nonchalance. 'The ones you speak of know nothing.'

'Safeguard our secrets,' Rees said simply. 'That is my command.'

Tate bowed his head, as though in obeisance to a god. 'Be assured I shall act at once,' he promised. 'They shall not see the light of another dawn.'

By his side, Scully rubbed his hands in anticipation, looking forward to another killing: it had, after all, been such a long time. But when Sam Rees spoke, Scully was disappointed.

'No,' he said, 'we must first discover how close they have come to learning of our plans. Knowledge in the wrong hands can be deadly.'

'I am certain that they know nothing, my lord,' Tate said.

'All our lives will come to nothing if we do not stop them now,' Rees decided, and then dismissed Tate and Scully.

When they had gone, he turned to Millicent, acknowledging her presence for the first time. After a long, chilling silence, he spoke to her:

'You know who I am?'

Millicent nodded, but chose not to look into Rees' startling blue eyes, as if by doing so she would soak up some of his great evil, and become corrupted.

'How do you know of my identity?' Rees demanded, and now the force of his will was so powerful that Millicent had to meet his gaze. They exchanged looks, and each recognised the other for what they were. After all, the likes of them had been enemies from long before the dawn of time itself.

'Yes, I reasoned that it was you,' Rees said finally. 'I am glad that we finally meet, face-to-face, before the end of the Old . . . The New will be resplendent: the return of Order to Chaos!'

Millicent winced at Sam Rees' words. She knew what his order would be: the 'order' of Caligula and of Herod, of Hitler and of Stalin, and of all tyrants down through the ages. The order of Lucifer himself.

'Sadly you will not be present to witness my ascent,' Sam Rees told her. 'Your quest has been in vain . . . Tell me of the others.'

Millicent found the courage to stare directly into Sam Rees' eyes – a deed which had been unheard of for thousands upon thousands of years – and refused to answer.

'Who are they?' There was a hint of anger in Rees' voice now, as he experienced opposition to his will.

'I will not answer.' Millicent's voice was soft and gentle; and yet the power behind it was almost as strong as Rees' own.

'You will answer!'

'I will not.' The reply was unequivocal, a gauntlet thrown down before Rees.

'Then you will die.'

There was no fear now in Millicent's voice. 'Killing me means nothing,' she said. 'Others will follow in my footsteps. The likes of you are always defeated in the end.'

Rees sneered, and turned his full gaze on to Millicent. His eyes glowed red with unearthly fire and Millicent was surrounded by bands of energy which circled her, like so many bees waiting for the right moment to sting. A strange fog, as cold as ice, surrounded her, enveloping her in its freezing touch.

When the fog had dispersed, Millicent F. Rutherford had disappeared, banished forever from this world by the man some knew as Sam Rees.

Ami and Megabyte sat on the banks of the Thames, gazing forlornly into the waters. Adam had been gone almost an hour now, and they were just starting to get worried, when he suddenly crept up behind him. His face was dirty and his clothes were torn.

'What kept you?' Megabyte asked grumpily.

'I was attacked,' he said, and added wryly. 'By a cat . . .'

When Adam had thrown himself under the parked car, he had rolled right under it to the other side. When the petrol tank had exploded he had been thrown clear of the blast, where he had landed in a doorway, out of view to the cat. It had been a lucky escape; if Adam had believed in such things he would have said that he had had some guardian angel watching over him in that deserted alley. Too weak to teleport, he had walked the whole way back from the East End.

'Where's Millicent?' Ami asked anxiously.

'I lost them,' Adam admitted. 'It was like they vanished into thin air . . .'

'But that's impossible . . .' Ami said. 'What's happened to Millicent? How come she got arrested?'

Adam shook her head. 'Whoever took Millicent, it wasn't the police,' he said.

'You mean she was kidnapped?' Ami asked, the panic obvious in her voice. Adam nodded, even though he couldn't explain why Millicent had willingly let herself be led away by the two men, who, from Ami and Megabyte's description, he guessed to be Tate and Scully. It sounded as though she had almost been expecting to be seized; as though her 'arrest' had been planned, part of the natural order of things. But planned by whom? And part of the natural order of which things?

'Somebody must be real nervous of what she's doing here,' Adam said.

'She sure made *me* nervous,' Megabyte quipped.

'Or else they're scared of what she knows . . .' he continued, and found his gaze being drawn to Cleopatra's Needle, like a magnet is drawn to iron. Beyond the obelisk, on the horizon, the afternoon sun shone off one of the brand new skyscrapers which had recently appeared in the Docklands. 'The answer's here somewhere!' he said, and slapped his fist into the palm of his other hand in a fit of frustration. 'It's probably staring us right in the face!'

'I just wish we had some more information,' Ami said. 'What else was on that postcard Millicent gave you?'

'Not much . . .' Adam reached into his hip pocket and pulled out the picture postcard which had been crumpled in his encounter with the cat. He glanced at it again: just the same familiar picture of Temple Hall.

'There's nothing here,' he said, and turned the card over to read the few words scribbled on its back. 'Just her home address, and the highly original message: "Wish you were here" . . .'

Ami grabbed the card from Adam. 'That's it!' she

exclaimed, and read the address. 'M.F. Rutherford, 77 Gabriel Walk, London SE10! That's what she meant!'

Megabyte took the card from her. 'At last a break! C'mon, guys, let's go.'

All three of them stood up to leave. As they did so, Ami glanced over in the distance at the tallest of the Docklands skyscrapers. The pyramid at its top glittered in the afternoon sunlight; it had an almost hypnotic affect on her and she realised just how much it resembled Cleopatra's Needle. She felt a dull sense of foreboding.

She shook her head, and looked across the Thames at a building on the other Embankment. The large clock on its tower read 12.30. 'Guys, you're not going to believe this, but I've got to go shopping . . .'

'*Shopping?*' Megabyte couldn't believe what he was hearing. 'But Millicent might be in danger.'

'I'm sorry, guys,' Ami said, 'but I promised my mum. She's got this big thing about buying me a birthday present, and – '

'I never knew it was your birthday,' Adam said.

'It's tomorrow,' Ami said. 'I'll catch up with you later, OK? And good luck.'

'Sure . . .' Adam said. Something was wrong here; otherwise, why were danger bells ringing so loudly in his head?

'Buy something nice,' Megabyte said, as Ami started to move off. 'And expensive! After all, that's what parents are for!'

Adam thoughtfully watched her walk away. This wasn't like Ami, he decided, to let her friends and Millicent down just for the chance of a simple shopping expedition. It was almost as if . . .

Adam shook his head. *Lighten up!* he told himself. *Why don't you just face the facts that never in your entire life are you ever going to understand women and their priorities!*

If Adam hadn't 'lightened up' at that moment he might have seen the white cat waiting at the kerbside which started to pad silently after Ami . . .

. . . The man known to some as Sam Rees chuckled, as he stared deep into his glass pyramid and watched Ami leave her friends. The girl's mind was complicated and strong-willed, as were the minds of all her confounded species, but it had still been a relatively simple matter for him to implant the suggestion into her mind. As simple as moving chess-pieces across a board, Sam Rees realised.

Sam Rees relished the irony of it all. A simple shopping trip, a mother's loving treat for her only daughter's birthday.

It was the last birthday Ami would ever know. Soon, she and her friends would be dead, and no-one would stand between Sam Rees and power beyond all imaginings.

Chapter Seven

'This is Gabriel Walk?' Megabyte asked in disbelief.

Adam checked his old copy of the London A-Z, and nodded. 'That's what it says here,' he said, uncertainly.

'It's a dump!' Megabyte decided, as indeed it was. Gabriel Walk was nothing but a pile of rubble somewhere in the wrong part of South-East London, on the banks of a foul-smelling and filthy canal. There had been houses here once, before they had been knocked down as part of the slum clearance programme, and before businessmen had discovered that they had no money to develop the site. Now Gabriel Walk was an eyesore, just another reminder of the urban blight which was sweeping through this particular part of London.

'This is where Gabriel Walk used to be before they tore it down,' Adam said.

Megabyte looked at the address on the back of Millicent's postcard. 'So where did Number 77 use to be?'

Adam's face lit up as he looked down at the canal: it was empty save for one dilapidated houseboat, painted in garish colours. He ran down to the quayside; on the side of the boat someone had painted the number 77 in glossy white paint. Adam reached out a hand: the paint was still wet.

'This has got to be it!' Megabyte said sarcastically, and joined Adam in jumping on deck. 'Who else but Millicent F. Rutherford would live in a dump like this?'

'I like it,' Adam said approvingly, and admired the colourful flowers and weird symbols painted around the prow of the boat.

'You would,' Megabyte said sadly – in matters of good taste he'd always considered Adam to be something of a no-hoper. He crossed over to a porthole to look inside the boat. Millicent had drawn the curtains, and he could see nothing; when he went to the hatch which led down into the boat he found that too was locked.

'I'll bet she's got all kinds of interesting things in there,' Adam said, as he peered through another porthole: that was also curtained off. 'She might have a notebook or a diary. Something that might help us.'

'Then let's teleport inside and find out,' Megabyte suggested. Adam nodded and they vanished in a crackle of energy, as he and Megabyte broke down their bodies' atoms to reconfigure them within Millicent F. Rutherford's wooden houseboat.

Mrs Jackson was despairing of ever finding anything which might please her daughter and make a suitable birthday present. She and Ami had been walking around the stalls and shops of trendy Covent Garden for almost two hours now and still Ami hadn't come across anything that she really liked. Or at least anything that was affordable, Mrs Jackson realised wryly.

Deciding to call it a day, Mrs Jackson suggested that they take advantage of a nearby pizzeria's all-you-can-eat-for-£5 offer. As she took Ami's hand, and led her away they passed a jewellery stall. Huge chunks of costume jewellery – pendants, necklaces, earrings and bracelets – glittered and twinkled invitingly in the afternoon sun. Ami stopped and dragged her mother over to the stall.

'Don't tell me that you've found something you like!' Mrs Jackson said incredulously, as Ami reached out and picked up one particular pendant.

Attached to a leather thong, it was about the size of a fifty-pence piece and was made out of some dull weathered slate-coloured stone. There was an irregular seven sided shape on it, picked out in faded gold, and in the centre there twinkled a tiny rhinestone. Ami's eyes opened wide in wonder, and she smiled: it was one of the most beautiful things she had ever seen, and she told her mother so.

Mrs Jackson took the pendant from Ami, and examined it with the expert eye of a woman who had never in her life been short-changed in a shop or had had palmed off on her a dodgy piece of merchandise.

'It's very unusual, darling,' she said approvingly, and rubbed her fingers over the stone. 'You've got good taste – just like your mother.' She turned to the stall holder, and offered him ten pounds for it. The stallholder pulled a face, indicating that the pendant was worth at least twice that amount, but Mrs Jackson stuck to her offer. Recognising that he'd met his match, the stallholder gave in, and accepted Mrs Jackson's profferred ten-pound note.

'Can I try it on now?' Ami asked, sounding like a little girl again, eager to play with a new toy. Her mother shook her head.

'This is for tomorrow and your birthday,' she said firmly. 'At least give your old mother the pleasure of wrapping it up, OK?'

Meekly Ami nodded, and followed her mother to the pizzeria. Neither of them thought to turn around and look back at the stallholder. If they had done they would have seen Scully leering evilly at them. Chuckling to himself, he bent down to stroke the white cat that was rubbing against his ankles . . .

Adam and Megabyte teleported into Millicent's houseboat – and straight into an impossibility, which confounded every one of their six senses. Inside they had expected to find chintzy and run-down furniture, maybe a few pots and pans hanging over a small kitchenette, and the remains of this morning's breakfast.

What they found instead was nothing. No furniture, no books, no trace whatsoever of Millicent F. Rutherford. Or of anything.

Within the houseboat there was precisely nothing. No Thing. No Place. No Time. No Where. Just a vast stretch of whiteness, streaming out into the distance as far as the eye could see. They looked down at their feet: there was no floor. They reached out their arms: nothing visible or invisible could be touched. Adam and Megabyte had teleported into an Absence of Everything, into a white and featureless void.

'Am I going mad?' Megabyte said, and his voice echoed eerily in the whiteness. 'First we were outside the houseboat, and then we teleported inside . . .' An irrational fear took hold of him. 'Adam, did we do something wrong? Are we dead?'

Adam shook his head slowly. 'We're not dead, Megabyte,' he said. 'Confused maybe . . . but not dead . . .'

'We blew it,' Megabyte said. 'We've come to the wrong place – wherever that is. I think we'd better get back to Gabriel Walk and try again.'

But when Adam and Megabyte vanished out of the void and back to the canalside, and then attempted to teleport a second time into Millicent's houseboat they found themselves back in the nothingness. Not understanding what was happening, they had to agree on one thing; Millicent F. Rutherford's 'home' was like no houseboat they had ever seen before.

There was a faint smell of roses in the air, and their bodies tingled with a strange energy.

This time, however, they were not alone. Waiting for them in the distance – about a quarter of a mile away, although it was hard to judge distance in the nothingness, were three figures. They waved to Adam and Megabyte and beckoned them over; the two Tomorrow People started to walk over to them.

'Holy guacomole,' Megabyte breathed when he had the chance to view the three figures up close.

The first was a man in his late forties, and at six and a half feet tall he towered over his companions. His face was heavily made up, and his pasty complexion and rosy cheeks reminded Megabyte of an actor in a third-rate pantomine. He was wearing the geeky uniform of an English schoolboy – cap, shorts, his striped tie askew, and his grubby shirt cuffs stained with ink blots.

Next to him stood an old-fashioned milk maid from out of a nursery rhyme, a fat, middle-aged woman with roly-poly arms and long blonde plaits. When she caught Adam and Megabyte looking at her she giggled shyly, and blushed, making her rouged cheeks even redder.

Their companion was stranger still. Although he seemed to be about the same age as his two colleagues, he was no more than three and a half feet in height, and was dressed from head to foot in red PVC rainwear and red wellington boots. By his side he carried a furled umbrella, with a duck's head handle.

He strode forwards – waddled would perhaps be the better word – and bowed low to the two boys. Adam and Megabyte couldn't help but smile: weird and disconcerting though they undoubtedly were, there was also something strangely comforting about the little man and his two companions.

Red Rainwear (as Adam and Megabyte had decided to call him) shook hands with them: for such a little man his handshake was surprisingly firm.

'Let me introduce my friends,' he piped in a reedy voice. 'Lizzie Motherwell –'

Adam reached out to shake the milkmaid's hand, but she giggled once more and turned shyly away.

'She doesn't say much, I'm afraid,' Red Rainwear sighed. 'She's what you might call pathologically shy, is our Mrs Motherwell.' He turned to the tall guy, dressed as a schoolboy. 'And this is my very good friend, Rupert Short.' Rupert reached down a hand for Adam and Megabyte to shake. 'He doesn't say much either.'

'Pathologically shy?' Megabyte ventured.

'No – he just doesn't have much to say.'

Adam turned back to Red Rainwear. 'Are you people all friends of Millicent's?' he asked.

The mention of Millicent seemed to animate the three strangers. 'Yes, and we're friends of yours too,' Red Rainwear said excitedly. 'Perhaps you can tell us where she's gone. We've not heard from her.'

‘We think she’s been kidnapped,’ Adam said. Lizzie and Rupert exchanged worried looks.

‘So it’s begun,’ Red Rainwear said, his voice full of foreboding. ‘Poor Millicent . . .’ He hung his head, and Megabyte could swear he saw a tear forming in the corner of the little man’s eye.

‘We don’t understand any of this,’ Adam said, gesturing around the white and formless void. ‘Can you help us?’

Red Rainwear regarded Adam and Megabyte for a second, as if debating whether he could trust them. Finally he said: ‘There are clever, *evil* people who are determined to stop us . . .’

‘What people!’ Megabyte demanded. ‘You’ve got to tell us whatever you know!’

‘Millicent’s in danger,’ Adam reminded them. ‘I think we can help, but we can’t help if we don’t know what we’re getting into. Trust us: we’re the good guys!’

Red Rainwear continued to stare at Adam and Megabyte but didn’t answer.

‘Millicent said that the future of the planet is in our hands,’ Adam continued. ‘What did she mean? Was she being serious?’

Red Rainwear looked over at Rupert and Lizzie; they nodded their heads.

‘Millicent is always serious,’ Red Rainwear said gravely. ‘She knows things and we have to listen to her.’

'That's what Ami said,' Adam remembered.

Red Rainwear looked interested, and urged Adam to continue.

'She said that she felt that Millicent was kinda special . . .'

Red Rainwear chuckled, and leant on his umbrella, rocking slowly back and forth. 'Millicent is special all right,' he said. 'Where is Ami now? If she's on her own she could be in terrible danger.'

'She's out with her mother shopping,' Megabyte said and frowned. 'What sort of danger?'

'Something monumental is going to happen.'

'Could you be a little more specific please?' Megabyte said wearily; he was getting a little tired of Red Rainwear's cryptic remarks.

'Trust nobody – except us, of course,' the little guy said, and the milkmaid and the schoolboy nodded their agreement. Red Rainwear raised his hand, and like a conjurer, produced a small piece of card out of thin air, which he handed to Adam.

It was a business card, on which were printed the words *The Zuzu Club*. There was no address or telephone number.

'You must go there – and quickly, too,' Red Rainwear told them. 'Someone has discovered the Rameses Cartouche.'

'And what the heck is the Rameses Cartouche?' Megabyte demanded.

'It's a cartouche that belonged to Rameses, of course.'

'Stupid me . . .'

'Rameses Ak'Hara, the tyrant Pharaoh of the Old Kingdom of Egypt, over four thousand years ago,' Red Rainwear explained. 'His burial chamber has never been found but the cartouche shows the way. It's a map: a key.'

'A key to what?' Adam asked.

'A key to understanding!'

Megabyte shook his head. 'Let me get this straight: something monumental is going to happen, but you don't know what it is, and you don't know when it's going to happen, or how to stop it. Am I right so far?'

Red Rainwear nodded, a little shamefacedly. If he had been allowed to tell Adam and Megabyte more, he would have done so; but there were certain laws that even he, Lizze Motherwell and Rupert Short were not permitted to transgress. Occasionally Millicent was allowed to break those rules; but then Millicent F. Rutherford was someone very special indeed.

'Follow the path before you,' Red Rainwear said mysteriously. 'There are no short cuts. Find the Cartouche – find the tomb. *Find out!*

And then Adam and Megabyte blinked, and Red Rainwear and his two companions were no longer there, and the only proof that Adam and Megabyte had not dreamt them was the card in Adam's hand.

The Zuzu Club. The Rameses Cartouche. What did it all mean?

Tate stared deep into the golden death-mask on the wall of Temple Hall. It glowed with an unearthly power, providing Tate with a direct telepathic link to his master, the one some knew as Sam Rees, but who Tate knew by a much older, and more secret name. Tate bowed his head in shame and fear: his lord was angry with him, and he knew the punishments Sam Rees was capable of meting out to those who failed him.

'Someone has discovered the Rameses Cartouche!' Sam Rees said, unconsciously echoing Red Rainwear's earlier words.

'Your greatness, I could never, never in my darkest dreams, have imagined the possibility of this coming to pass,' he said.

'My demands are clear,' Sam Rees said, communicating with his minion through the power of the ancient Egyptian mask. 'I ordered that the Cartouche was to be destroyed. Yet it still exists! Why did you disobey my orders?'

'My Lord, I did not disobey you,' Tate claimed. 'It was a matter of circumstance. I entrusted the task to another and he failed me.'

Tate's excuse had no effect on Sam Rees: 'The deed was entrusted to you. It was my will. And now my stupidity has jeopardised everything.'

Tate fell to his knees in front of the golden mask. 'Spare me, my Lord,' he begged. 'I am the architect of your New Kingdom. Please forgive your humble servant!'

‘I do not forgive,’ was Sam Rees’ implacable answer. ‘Now get up off your knees!’

Tate did as instructed, his heart suddenly full of hope. Surely if Sam Rees had meant him to die, he would by now be dead, a smouldering heap of ashes on the floor? Sam Rees had spared his unworthy life because he still had use of him.

‘Can it be mere ill luck that the Cartouche should come to light at this time?’ Tate asked. ‘I submit that there are other forces at work!’

In his sanctum, Sam Rees reflected for a moment, considering Tate’s image in the centre of his glass pyramid. ‘That may be so,’ he said finally. ‘So it is all the more important that you destroy it now.’

‘I live only to serve you, my Lord,’ Tate declared.

‘There may still be time,’ Sam Rees decided. ‘Destroy the Cartouche and those who seek it – or I will destroy you!’

Chapter Eight

Megabyte raised his eyes heavenwards and sighed. It was almost nine-thirty at night and he and Adam had spent the best part of two hours at Ami's house, trying to track down the Zuzu Club in the London phone directory.

When that had failed, they had tried Directory Enquiries, who had helpfully given them the number of a Zorba's doner kebab shop in Stoke Newington, but nothing else. Ami had joined in the hunt, searching through her *Time Out* directory of the latest and trendiest clubs in London but so far, in Megabyte's words, they had drawn 'one big fat zero'.

'Let's face it,' he said, at last. 'There is no Zuzu Club!'

Adam fingered the card Red Rainwear had given him. 'It's the only lead we have,' he said.

'Yeah, and look who gave it to us,' Megabyte reminded him. 'Would you let any of those Three Amigos back there out on their own, 'cause I sure wouldn't!'

'We can't give up,' Ami said. 'We have to find what's happened to Millicent.'

'Happy Birthday!'

Ami turned to the door and cringed. Her mother was walking into the living room, holding aloft a birthday cake on top of which she had placed a number of lighted candles.

'Mum, my birthday's tomorrow!' Ami protested.

'So picky, that girl!' Mrs Jackson complained, and nodded to Adam and Megabyte to clear a space on the table so she could put down the cake. 'I just thought that while your friends are here we could make a party of it!'

Ami rolled her eyes: sometimes her mother could be an ever bigger kid than she herself had ever been. Finally she gave in; there were certain powers in this world against which even Tomorrow People had no defence and Ami's mother was one of them. To congratulatory cheers from the others, she bent down and blew out the lighted candles.

'And now it's presents time!' Mrs Jackson said after she had cut up the cake and passed everyone a slice. She handed her daughter an elaborately wrapped package. 'You'll never guess what it is!'

Smiling, Ami unwrapped the present and took out the pendant. She held it up for everyone to see: the rhinestone in its centre glimmered in the light, like an eye, watching them all.

'Hey, that's really neat!' Megabyte approved, as

Ami slipped the pendant over her head. She felt its weight around her neck, felt its presence against her body; all her nerve-ends started to tingle, and a wonderful feeling of warmness washed over her body.

And then suddenly Ami leapt up from the table, knocking the birthday cake to the floor. There was a searing, white-hot pain in her solar plexus, just as if someone had kicked her in the stomach, and she doubled up in gut-wrenching pain.

Her mother, Adam and Megabyte were at her side instantly, but she pushed them away from her, and ran out of the room out into the hall, and up the stairs.

The world was spinning sickeningly around Ami and the pain had moved from her stomach to envelop now her entire body. Her head felt like it would burst, and her eyes flooded with tears of pain, as she staggered into her bedroom. She leant on her dressing room table, taking long deep breaths. Slowly the pain receded, and she raised her head. It was her imagination of course, but just for a second it seemed that the rhinestone in the centre of her pendant was glowing a deep and dangerous red.

She looked at her reflection in the mirror. For one-instant she saw not herself in the glass, but that of a man, of a man thousands of years old. His eyes burned into her very soul, and he smiled at her. Ami knew at that moment that they were bonded together, she and him, that his will was her will, and that she would do whatever he required of her.

That warm feeling swept over Ami's body again, and the pain ceased. Calmly she stroked the pendant and then slipped it out of sight down the front of her top. She was dimly aware of someone knocking at her bedroom door, and she walked over and opened it to greet the three worried faces of Adam, Megabyte and her mother.

'Ami, darling, are you all right?' her mother asked.

Ami looked at Mrs Jackson curiously, as if she couldn't understand what all the fuss was about.

'I'm fine,' she reassured her. 'I must have choked on a piece of cake, that's all. Now, shall we carry on with the party?'

The party continued for another hour, and Adam and Megabyte soon forgot about Ami's sudden fit. Yet when they looked at her there was a strange glazed look in her eyes, as if she wasn't quite there. When Megabyte had mentioned, over a final game of Trivial Pursuit, that she seemed to be a thousand miles away, Ami had just shrugged, told him not to be so stupid, and had then gone on to win the game.

It was nearing eleven o'clock, and Mrs Jackson had retired to bed half an hour ago, when the phone rang. It was for Megabyte, his father responding to the message Megabyte had left on the ansaphone earlier that evening. Megabyte snatched a piece of paper from the note pad by the telephone and scribbled down an address. He grunted his thanks to his dad, replaced the receiver and turned to Adam and Ami with a triumphant grin.

'What d'you know?' he said. 'My old man just came up trumps! There is a Zuzu Club, in Cairo, Egypt.'

Adam stood up. 'I should've thought of that,' he said. 'It's kinda obvious.'

'You can't get it right all the time, can you, Adam?' Megabyte said gleefully and leapt to his feet as well. 'OK, do we go?'

'No. It's a waste of time.'

Adam and Megabyte both turned to Ami, who was shaking her head sadly.

'It's the only lead we've got,' Megabyte pointed out.

'We could go tomorrow, couldn't we?' she asked weakly. 'There's no great hurry.'

Adam regarded Ami strangely. He had never seen her behave like this before. She had been so concerned with tracking Millicent down: was she now going to let her new friend down?

'I think we should go now,' he said gently. 'But if you're not feeling well, you stay here and we'll go.'

'I don't want you to go!' Ami shouted angrily. 'How many times have I to say it?' She raised her hands to her forehead and massaged her temples; she had a terrible headache. 'It's dangerous,' she said, her voice calmer now. 'You'll die there.'

Adam reached out for Ami's hand to reassure her:

it was oddly cold to the touch, and he wondered whether she was sickening for something.

'We'll be OK,' he promised her. 'You don't look well. Go to bed and get some sleep.'

'I'm fine, OK?' Ami snapped. The voice in her head was stronger now, and it was becoming harder and harder to resist its commands.

'C'mon, we've got to go, Adam!' Megabyte hurried him on. Reluctantly Adam agreed, and with a farewell wave at Ami he vanished along with Megabyte.

As soon as they had gone, Ami sank back into her seat and buried her face in her hands, and sobbed. The voice in her head was so strong now that she could hardly hear herself think. It boomed throughout her mind, bending her will to its commands, denying her any form of self-control or free will. Around her neck the pendant started to glow again.

– *Who are they?* the voice of Sam Rees echoed in her brain. *What are their names?*

– Adam. Megabyte. Ami replied, and frowned. Once upon a time those were the names of her friends. But now the only friend she had was Sam Rees.

– *And what do they know of my plans?*

– Very little. Almost nothing.

– This pleases me. I am anxious that they learn nothing more. You know what you must do?

Ami nodded, and licked her lips, as Sam Rees,

through the power of the stone that Ami wore around her neck, twisted and perverted her mind, instilling in her a frightening blood lust.

– *I must kill them, my Lord*, Ami intoned over and over again like some sort of obscene mantra. – *I must kill them both.*

And what was more she was even looking forward to it . . .

Chapter Nine

The Zuzu Club was a seedy run-down joint in one of the less salubrious districts of the Egyptian capital. When Adam and Megabyte arrived the club was locked; as Megabyte said, that was all to their advantage. If the club was closed there would be no one to interfere with their snooping around.

Once they had teleported inside, they could see that, if anything, the club was seedier inside than out. Shabby chairs had been piled up on the rickety tables, and the tatty carpet was marked with wine stains and cigarette burns. In one corner of the room there stood an old scratched piano which had plainly not been played for a long time, and a few garish posters had been taped to the walls.

Along one wall, there ran a bar which, during open hours, served cheap, strong spirits and liqueurs. Several half-empty glasses were there, obviously waiting to be cleared up in the morning.

'OK, let's get logical,' Megabyte began as his eyes adjusted to the darkness. 'Where would you want to put a cartouche – ' A sudden thought hit him. 'Hey, what is a cartouche anyway.'

'It's an Egyptian tablet, usually made of stone and with inscriptions and hieroglyphics written on it,' Adam said airily. 'I looked the word up in the encyclopedia before we went around to Ami's.'

'You would have,' Megabyte said. He bet Adam was the sort of person who knew bus timetables by heart as well. 'OK. Where would you want to hide a priceless Egyptian treasure? Someplace safe, huh?'

'Thank you, Sherlock Holmes,' Adam said sarcastically, and then froze, as a shaft of light lit up the room and a door in the far wall slowly opened. Adam and Megabyte both pressed themselves against the wall, hiding in the shadows.

An unshaven, weasely-looking Egyptian dressed in a scruffy cream suit enetered the main bar area and looked suspiciously around. Adam and Megabyte exchanged anxious glances: had he heard them moving about?

Thankfully, just as the newcomer was about to cross over the room and switch on the main light, a telephone rang. He cursed to himself in Egyptian, and returned to his office to answer the phone. Keeping to the shadows, Adam and Megabyte crept after him and looked through the open doorway into the office.

'You want to make me an offer?' the man rapped into the receiver, and smiled. He opened the drawer to his desk, and took out a large object, wrapped up in a dazzlingly colourful Egyptian shroud: this was obviously the subject of his business discussion. 'If you're serious then you'll need to move real fast on this one. Just give me your top price – I've no time for haggling. I've other buyers waiting for this one . . .'

As the man continued his negotiations on the phone, it became apparent to Adam and Megabyte that he was a black marketeer, a dealer in stolen Egyptian antiques, and probably a smuggler as well. If anyone might have the Rameses Cartouche then it would be him. He finished his deal on the phone, and replaced the receiver. As he did so, there was a loud knocking at the front door of the club. Cursing once more, he left his office and went back into the bar area to open up.

Adam and Megabyte took their chance. As soon as the dealer had gone, they sneaked into his office. Megabyte tugged at the desk drawer, but the dealer had locked it when we went to answer the door.

'That's got to be the Cartouche!' Adam said.

'So what's it doing in a dump like this?' Megabyte asked, and then froze as they heard the distinctive voice of Scully, as the dealer reluctantly admitted him and Tate into the club.

'We can see that your establishment is closed for business, Mister Roach,' Scully said, as he entered the club. He cracked the knuckles of his hands, breaking the silence in the bar. 'We, however, are here on business of a different kind.'

'Which is?' Roach asked, feigning ignorance. He watched Scully carefully, as he strode around the bar area, acting as if he owned the place.

'Let's just say that we are very interested in obtaining a certain cartouche that happens to be in your possession.' Scully's voice was pleasant and polite; it was at times such as this that he was at his most dangerous.

'I don't know what you're talking about,' Roach claimed.

'The Rameses Cartouche, Mister Roach,' Tate said, ignoring Roach's protestations of ignorance. 'Mister Scully and I have no time to waste. I will of course pay you: shall we say one million dollars?'

Roach snorted contemptuously. 'A million's not even in the frame,' he scoffed. 'I think it's worth just a little bit more than that, don't you?'

'Money is no object,' Tate said. 'I will pay you whatever you ask. Bring it here!'

Scully strode up to Roach and grabbed him menacingly around the neck. 'Do it! Now! Get the cartouche!'

Roach paused for a moment, and then nodded meekly. He turned and walked slowly into his office; and then slammed and locked the door behind him, just as Adam and Megabyte hid themselves out of sight behind a beaded curtain. They watched as

Roach raced over to his desk and unlocked the drawer, taking out the priceless cartouche, still wrapped in its ceremonial shroud.

Roach cast a nervous look behind him at the door; he could hear Scully pounding on it and he knew that it would only be a matter of seconds before he burst the lock. Clutching the cartouche close to his chest, he climbed out of the ground floor window, just as Scully smashed the door down.

Scully took in the situation in an instant, and headed for the window, racing after Roach. Left alone in the room, Tate paused for a second while, behind the beaded curtain, Adam and Megabyte held their breath. Tate frowned, as though somehow sensing the presence of the two Tomorrow People, and then shook his head, realising that the fulfilment of his master's wishes should be his only concern for the moment.

As soon as Tate had disappeared Adam and Megabyte left their hiding place. If they were to get the Rameses Cartouche before Tate and Scully then there wasn't a moment to lose.

Roach ran through the darkened alleyways of Cairo heading for the old part of town. This wouldn't be the first time that he had had to make a speedy retreat from his headquarters: in the world of international art smuggling there were some who would stop at nothing to get their hands on some of the treasures he'd stolen.

Yet there was something strange about those two who had turned up tonight. The younger man – Scully, he'd heard him called – was a nasty piece of work, the strong-arm man of the operation; Roach had no doubt that he'd find great pleasure ripping him apart limb from limb if he caught him. But it was the older man who really scared Roach; he knew that Tate would do anything to get the Cartouche.

Not that Roach had any idea why Tate and Scully wanted the Cartouche. Sure, he reasoned to himself, it was a nice piece of work, but hardly worth more than a couple of million. Still, a million was a million.

He arrived at a fork in the road and debated which one to take. In the distance he could hear footsteps rattling after him, and he took the left-hand fork, running down the narrow alleyway as if all the hounds of hell were after him – as, indeed, they were.

The alleyway debouched into a crossroads, and Roach heard two voices shouting to each other. 'Adam! He's down here,' he heard someone say in an American accent. Assuming that Tate and Scully had been joined by other accomplices, Roach spun on his heels in the opposite direction – and ran straight into Scully.

Scully grinned down at him and grabbed at his windpipe, sinking his pincer-like fingers deep into Roach's neck. He pushed Roach face-first into a brick wall so violently that Roach felt his nose crack as it hit the brick. Warm, sticky blood started to flow freely from his nostrils.

'You said you'd pay!' Roach blubbered. 'We had a deal! You guys have got no sense of honour.'

Scully delivered a sharp jab to his side and Roach doubled up, falling to the ground in pain.

'Honour?' Tate, who had joined them, spat out the word, as he watched Roach writhe about the ground in agony. 'Such fine words dribbling from the lips of a jackal such as you.' He nodded to Scully, who bent down and took the wrapped Cartouche from the inside pocket of Roach's cream jacket, now stained the dark red of spilt blood.

Adam and Megabyte arrived just in time to see Scully advance menacingly on the recumbent Roach. They stayed hidden in the shadows and watched Scully as he grinned and flexed his hands, and approached the helpless black marketeer; whatever he had planned for Roach it was clear that he was going to enjoy it.

'Who are you people?' Roach asked, and gagged on the blood running from his nose.

'That is not your concern,' Tate said.

'Be reasonable,' Roach begged although he knew that his end was near. 'I have contacts. I can sell that thing for millions. We can be partners. I – '

Roach spoke no more, and, from their vantage

point, Adam and Megabyte turned away in horror and revulsion, as Scully struck at the helpless Roach, and delivered him up to the gods of Ancient Egypt.

Soon the whole of the alleyway reeked of the cloying and terrible stench of death by sacrifice . . .

Chapter Ten

It was one o'clock in the morning in Cairo when Tate and Scully entered the lobby of the plush colonial-style hotel. Although it was late, the reception area was still busy with tourists who had just arrived from Cairo's international airport. To say that Tate and Scully made an impressive entrance would be an understatement. Their clothes were dishevelled as a result of their chasing the unfortunate Roach down some of the seedier alleyways of Cairo's old town, and Scully's usually immaculate suit was stained with dirt and freshly-spilt blood.

The white-suited desk clerk looked warily at the two ne'er-do-wells, as Tate sauntered up to the reception desk and demanded, in fluent Arabic, a suite facing the pyramids. The clerk considered calling hotel security, but instead claimed that all the hotel's rooms were fully booked for the weekend. Tate produced a fat roll of dollar bills from his pocket – the clerk's expert eye judged that there were at least two thousand there – and produced an immediate change in the clerk's attitude. Of course, the esteemed gentlemen could have the very best suite in the hotel, he smarmed; the most excellent view of the Pyramids and the River Nile that there was to be had. And if Sir would just sign the register than he would personally see to it that their baggage was taken to their room.

Tate gruffly replied that they had no baggage, just the small hold-all he was carrying, and that they would be leaving first thing tomorrow morning. The clerk raised an eyebrow, but said nothing; when his guests paid in advance, and in cash, he never asked too many awkward questions.

As Tate and Scully signed the register in the names of Messrs D. Lawrence and M. Holloway (after all, they couldn't afford to be too careful), they didn't notice Adam and Megabyte who entered by the main doors, and immediately hid themselves behind a large potted palm tree. Adam peeked his head out, trying to see what was going on and straining to hear the conversation between the desk clerk and Tate and Scully.

'Your suite has one of the most commanding views in all Cairo, sir,' he could hear the clerk saying effusively. 'Film stars and other celebrities have sung its praises many times.'

Tate wasn't interested in such details, as he signed his false name with a flourish of his pen. 'All I am concerned about is the Pyramids,' he said. 'The room does have a view of the Pyramids, does it not?'

'They rise like mountains in the distance, sir,' the clerk cooed, and picked up a room key from the board behind him. 'Suite 501 is the finest room in all Cairo.'

'That's as it should be,' Tate approved, and started to walk toward the elevator with Scully, passing the potted palm behind which Adam and Megabyte had been hiding. Tate paused for a moment, sensing a certain tingling of discharged energy in the air, and looked uncertainly at the palm tree. Its leaves were swaying gently as if in an invisible wind. But when he looked behind it there was nothing to be seen.

Dismissing his suspicions, Tate followed Scully to the waiting elevator.

In a flash of blue Adam and Megabyte materialised ahead of Tate and Scully in Suite 501, a luxurious series of rooms which, as the desk clerk had promised, enjoyed a magnificent view of the Great Pyramids. Megabyte let out a loud whistle of appreciation.

'Some classy joint, huh?' he said and went over to the open window. Below them, glistening in the light of the full moon, a large river meandered through the town. 'I guess that's the river Nile?'

'Can we leave the sightseeing for another day?' Adam said urgently. 'We need to find somwhere to hide before Tate and Scully get here. He bundled

Megabyte off into the ensuite bathroom just as he heard Scully place his keys in the door.

Tate strode first into the room, clutching his hold-all to his side, as if it contained the greatest treasure in the world. He walked over to the window, and nodded approvingly at the view, before instructing Scully to lock the door. From a crack through the half-closed bathroom door Adam and Megabyte watched.

Satisfied that they were safe, Tate unzipped the hold-all and took out the still-shrouded Cartouche and carefully unwrapped it. He caressed it, as one might a lover, with eyes full of emotion.

Scully scowled, impatient for their work to be finished; if the truth were to be known he didn't like being so near to the Great Pyramids: for some reason they gave him, the creeps, as if all the gods of Ancient Egypt were watching down on them disapprovingly. He wasn't quite sure whether he believed in them or not, but he certainly knew that he had no wish whatsoever to face their wrath.

Tate noticed Scully's concern, smiled indulgently, and then laid the Cartouche on a long table which faced the window and the view of the Pyramids. He went over to the window, and slid it open; a soft summer breeze blew into the room.

'You must realise, my friend, that, for me, the Rameses Cartouche bears a profound significance,' Tate begun. 'You cannot hope to understand why, or how much. Truly I believe to rescue the Cartouche from unnecessary destruction: that is why I chose to conceal it deep beneath the shifting sands of the remotest desert. I could never have foreseen its untimely discovery, by people such as Roach.'

'We must destroy it now,' Scully insisted.

Tate sadly agreed, and, with a sigh, ordered Scully to extinguish the lights of the room. From the bathroom Adam and Megabyte heard the striking of a match as Tate lit two tall candles which he had taken from his hold-all and placed on either side of the Cartouche at the centre of the table. The older man knelt down before the makeshift altar, and opened his arms wide to the night sky, as if he was trying to gather the whole of the Great Pyramids of Egypt within his grasp.

'O, Pyramids of Egypt forgive me!' he declaimed in a voice which sent shivers down Adam and Megabyte's spines. 'Bear witness, O great Osiris, to the woe which wells within my soul.'

Adam looked at Megabyte – *We've got to do something, fast!* he said.

They watched, fascinated, as Tate stood up and wrapped the sacred Rameses Cartouche in its ceremonial shroud again.

'In the name of Anubis and of Horus, I sanctify this deed – a blessed sacrifice for the greater glory of the New Kingdom – and shall commemorate it, from this day on, forever more!'

Tate threw back his head, as though in ecstasy, and muttered a prayer in Ancient Egyptian. It was a prayer that had not been heard on the surface of this planet for over four thousand years.

Outside in the warm Egyptian night came the sound of approaching thunder. From somewhere far away streaks of lightning illuminated the sky. The atmosphere in Suite 501 was suddenly electric with the approach of the elemental forces called into being by Tate.

Adam looked at Tate: his eyes were still closed. Scully was close beside him, standing by a small coffee table. On the glass top of the coffee table there was an onyx ashtray, which he judged to be roughly the same size and weight of the Rameses Cartouche. He turned back to Megabyte.

– *I've got an idea,* Adam told him – *It's crazy but it could work. Knock on the door!*

– What d'you mean?

– Just teleport outside and knock on the door!

Impressed by the urgency of Adam's thoughts, Megabyte didn't ask any more but did as he was told. With a surge of concentration he transported himself into the corridor outside Tate's room, and rapped smartly on the door.

Tate opened his eyes, and he growled, angry that his ritual had been disturbed by this unwelcome intrusion. Muttering an Egyptian curse which, like his prayer, had not been heard from thousands of years, he despatched Scully to see who it was.

'Ignore it,' Scully suggested.

'See who it is!' Tate repeated. 'No one must be allowed to disturb the ceremony! Everything must go according to plan!'

Scully suppressed his frustration and anger, and did Tate's bidding. But when he opened the door there was no one there (which was hardly surprising as Megabyte had teleported himself back into the bathroom as soon as Scully had opened the door). The long corridor outside Suite 501 was empty; and there was no place where anyone could have hidden.

'What is it?' Tate called over, sensing Scully's confusion. 'What is wrong?'

'Something strange is going on,' Scully said. Tate sighed, and walked across the room to join Scully by the open door.

Adam seized his chance, and rushed out of the bathroom and into the main room. He glanced at the doorway: both Tate and Scully had stepped out into the corridor to see if they could spot who had been pounding on the door. With his heart beating madly, he snatched the Rameses Cartouche out of its ceremonial shroud, and replaced it with the onyx ashtray, wrapping the shroud around that.

Flashing a mental message to Megabyte to join him, Adam vanished from Suite 501, just as Tate and Scully returned to the room. They had spotted a drunk rolling down the corridor looking for his room, and that had been explanation enough for Tate.

He returned to his makeshift altar, and resumed his obeisances to all the dark and dangerous gods of Ancient Egypt, with Scully watching on as a fascinated and slightly fearful acolyte. As Tate paid homage to the elemental powers, the candles on the altar started to flicker, and the thunder resumed its distant and menacing rumbling, and the lightning flashed once more in the weirdly cloudless sky.

Tate seemed now to have fallen into a trance as he zeroed all his concentration on to what he supposed was still the Rameses Cartouche wrapped up in its shroud. He channelled all the dark powers of the night into his own being. He called on the might of Seth, the god of storms, and of Anubis and Horus, lords of the dead; he drew down the might of Bubastis, the cat-goddess, and of Sekhmet, the unrelenting Queen of War; he dared to name Amon-Ra, himself, lord of all creation and the fire of the sun.

A bolt of eldritch lightning burst in through the open window and struck the 'Cartouche', which burst into a shower of flames. At that point Tate's eyes snapped open, and he looked sadly down at the pile of ashes on the table.

'It is done,' he whispered in the now unearthly silence. 'The Rameses Cartouche is no more and the danger to our plans has passed . . .'

It was early morning in Cairo, when Adam and Megabyte sat down at a table in the corner of a run-down café on the edge of a busy market place and ordered two mint teas. On the table before them was a pile of guide books which Adam had bought from the local bookshop as soon as it had opened: Megabyte picked up one of the titles: *The Idiot's Guide to Egypt*.

'That's one for you,' Adam said nonchalantly.

'Cheap shot, Adam,' Megabyte said, and gave him a friendly, but not-so-gentle punch in the ribs. He took the Cartouche from him, taking care that no one else in the café could see what they were looking at.

The Rameses Cartouche was indeed beautiful, bearing intricate patterns and hieroglyphics as well as a design which resembled a seven-pointed star. Megabyte guessed that museums across the world would pay millions to have this in their collection. He wondered what Amanda James back in London would say if she could see what he was holding in his hands now: that'd knock that smug expression off her face, he decided with glee.

Adam took the Cartouche back and stared at it, as if by doing that it would reveal its secrets to him. But psychometry – the art of receiving images and vibrations from inanimate objects – was not a psychic talent that Adam had yet developed, and the Cartouche remained stubbornly 'silent'.

'Remember what Red Rainwear said?' Adam asked Megabyte, and the red-haired American groaned, as he recalled the three weirdoes they had met inside Millicent's 'houseboat'.

'Only you and me could get mixed up with guys like that,' he cackled ironically.

'Even so, everything he's said so far has turned out to be true,' Adam reminded him. 'He said the cartouche was a map, a key to understanding . . .' He turned the Cartouche thoughtfully over in his hands, while Megabyte idly flipped through his *Idiot's Guide*.

On the top side of the Cartouche there was embossed an oval shape, filled with heiroglyphics, the meaning of which was lost on Adam. Adam reached out for one of the other guide books, checked a reference in the index, and then flicked to the appropriate page.

'"The cartouche is an archetypal symbol of Kingship",' he read out loud. '"It is an oval of rope that contained the hieroglyphs of the Pharaoh's Nomen and Prenomen, Horus Name, Nebty Name and Golden Horus Name . . ."' He stared up blankly from the book, and looked at Megabyte, who shook his head sympathetically.

'Now be honest with me,' said Megabyte. 'Did you really understand a single word of that?'

Adam shook his head, and laid the Cartouche on the table, between their mint teas.

'Let's face it, Adam, we're way out of our depth here. Let's go home, back to Ami . . .'

Adam banged his fist on the table in frustration. 'It

can't be that complicated!' he cried. 'But it's just not a map!'

Megabyte picked up the Cartouche, and turned it over and over in his hand. Adam was right, the hei-roglyphics on its face meant nothing to him. For all that they had to tell, they might as well have been the scratches on the obverse of the tablet.

Scratches? Megabyte looked more closely at the bottom face of the Cartouche. He pointed the scratchmarks out to Adam, and then picked up his *Idiot's Guide*. He turned to a map of Cairo.

'That's no scratchmark!' he said, and pointed to a long groove on the Cartouche. 'Well, I mean it is a scratchmark but – ' He pushed the *Idiot's Guide* towards Adam and asked him to compare the scratchmark to one of the features of the map.

'Adam, it's the River Nile,' he said excitedly. 'I've just found your map scratched out on the back!'

Adam looked at the Cartouche, and then at the map and then at the Cartouche. Megabyte was right! The truth had been staring them in the face all the time but they had been too blind to see. He pointed out several small triangular indentations on the Cartouche.

'These triangles must be groups of pyramids,' he guessed. 'There are the big three in Cairo; and here's another bunch off to the West.' He traced his finger down to another group of seven pyramids to the south. The same heiroglyphics which were on the top face of the pyramid had been etched on here; one particular pyramid was singled out for special attention.

'Those hieroglyphics must spell Rameses Ak'Hara, the name of the Pharaoh. And this must mark his tomb: it's underneath the seventh pyramid!'

'So what do we do now?' Megabyte asked.

'What do you think?' Adam said. 'We go there. We find out what it is that everybody doesn't want us to find out about!'

Megabyte's face fell: this sounded like too much hard work. 'That's a heck of a lot of heavy digging under a pyramid, Adam,' he said pessimistically. 'You've got a spade?'

'Only idiots dig, Megabyte,' Adam said with a twinkle in his eye. 'Smart people teleport!'

They looked around to make sure that no one was watching them. Satisfied that the coast was clear, they teleported out of the café, en route to the long-lost pyramid of Rameses Ak'Hara.

But they were wrong: someone had seen them vanish from the café with the Rameses Cartouche. With her whole body consumed with hatred for Adam and Megabyte, and her heart filled with murder, Ami teleported off in pursuit of her former friends.

Around her neck the pendant of Sam Rees glowed as crimson as the blood of Adam and Megabyte that she would soon see flow . . .

Chapter Eleven

Adam and Megabyte teleported into absolute blackness, and for a second they both panicked. Then Adam remembered the battery torches they had bought in a Cairo street market before leaving and clicked his on, instructing Megabyte to do the same. For the first time in untold centuries light penetrated the forgotten tomb of Rameses Ak'Hara, dispelling the inky blackness which had enshrouded the place since the evil Pharaoh had been lain to rest.

They were in a tiny chamber, only about six feet square, which had been hewn out of the featureless rock. As their lights played over the walls, they each experienced a great sense of disappointment: the walls were bare, with no doorways, no means of either entering or exiting the place. If there ever had been doorways in this chamber, then they had long since been blocked up.

'So this is the fabulous tomb of Rameses the Unprouncable, huh?' Megabyte said sarcastically and his words fell dull and heavy in the confined atmosphere of the chamber. 'It looks to me that the repo men got here first.'

Adam shook his head, and looked around the chamber: four rock walls, no doorways leading to another part of the tomb, no hieroglyphic inscriptions on the wall, no evidence that human beings had ever stepped inside this narrow room.

'We must have got it wrong,' he said.

'Gimme a break, Adam! We followed the map directions on the Cartouche to the letter.' He shone his torch on to the tablet that Adam was holding in his hand. 'We're here – with just one more brick wall to bash our heads against! Let's get out of here.'

Adam didn't give up so easily. He looked down at the Cartouche, weighing it carefully in his hand. 'Red Rainwear said that the Cartouche was both a map and a key,' he recalled. He looked at the wall before him; there, just at face-level, there was a small indentation in the rock surface. He walked up to examine it more closely.

It was a small oblong slot, cut vertically into the wall. As Adam and Megabyte shone their torchlights on it, a tiny spider scuttled out of the slot. Adam looked down at the Cartouche: it was just as wide as the slot. Suddenly he realised that the Rameses Cartouche would fit it exactly, as easily as a key fitting into a lock. *A key*, Red Rainwear had said. Grinning at Megabyte, he inserted the Cartouche lengthways into the slot.

'Get outta my face!' Megabyte said, as soon as he realised what Adam was planning. 'You have just got to be kidding!'

Adam shot him a look which seemed to say: *Oh yeah? Then just watch this, buddy!* and turned the Rameses Cartouche in the slot.

Nothing happened. The chamber remained as silent as it had been for centuries, and Megabyte turned to Adam, with a know-it-all smile on his face.

'I told you that – Good grief, what's happening?'

The ground started to tremble beneath their feet, and handfuls of dust started to fall from the ceiling as machinery, unused for centuries, once more was put into operation. Suddenly the entire wall before them started to open out, a huge granite door, forcing Adam and Megabyte to press themselves against the opposite wall to avoid being crushed by its huge bulk. The door finally clunked to a halt and Adam and Megabyte stepped forwards into the room beyond.

The sight took their breath away. A massive chamber, about the size of a small house lay beyond the door, packed to the ceiling with fantastic golden treasures, designed to accompany the dead Pharaoh on his journey to the afterlife.

Religious writings covered the walls of the burial chamber, along with stylised pictures of incidents in the dead Pharaoh's life, in colours as bright and as vibrant as the day they had first been painted. In the centre of the chamber, dominating everything else, was a huge black sarcophagus, mounted on a dais.

'Er, Adam, this is just a wild guess but I'd say that this was it!' Megabyte said fliply, but even he was impressed. After all, he and Adam were the first people to step into the lost tomb of Rameses Ak'hara for over forty centuries.

'This is awesome,' Megabyte continued. 'And also deeply weird. This is not what I expected.'

'The Pharaohs believed that when they died their souls made a long voyage out to the stars,' he pointed up to the ceiling, which was covered with elaborate designs depicting the constellations.

'Adam, remind me what we're looking for,' Megabyte said.

'An answer.'

'That's what I thought. And do we have any idea what this answer might look like?'

'We'll know when we find it,' Adam said, sounding more confident than he actually felt. He walked over to the great stone sarcophagus in the centre of the chamber.

'What d'you reckon is in there?' Megabyte asked warily, even though he'd seen far too many late-night horror movies not to have a pretty good idea.

'It'll only be a body,' Adam said nonchalantly, as he looked around for something to prise the lid off the coffin. He picked up two spikes which had been left at the foot of the dais. 'What else would you expect to find in a tomb? And don't look so horrified: it'll be wrapped up in bandages.'

'What good's a bandage when you're dead?' Megabyte muttered, as he helped Adam lever the lid off the top of the sarcophagus.

Summoning up all their strength, Adam and Megabyte pushed at the lid of the sarcophagus until, with a mighty crash, it fell to the floor. Steeling themselves, they peered over the lid of the coffin to find –

– precisely nothing. The sarcophagus of Rameses Ak'Hara was empty.

'How can it be empty?' Adam said, and stood back from the sarcophagus. 'The guy died; he was buried. The tomb was shut behind him!'

'Sukaru!'

Their hearts missed a beat as they spun around on their heels. Hovering behind them in his familiar green haze was the figure of Tutankhamun.

Megabyte caught his breath. 'Kid, I wish you wouldn't keep doing that,' he complained, and cursed himself for being so jumpy in what was, after all, just another dark and murky tomb which hadn't been opened for over four thousand years, and whose dead occupant had decided to go walkabout.

'Sukaru! Amtoudi! Amtoudi!'

'Amtoudi again,' Megabyte said. 'What is it? What does it mean?'

Adam stepped forward, trying once more to reach

into Tutankhamun's mind. – *We need your help. Where do we go from here? What do we need to know? Where do we look?*

The boy-king seemed to understand, and he stretched out his arm to draw their attention to a series of paintings on a far wall of the chamber. Adam and Megabyte shone their torches on to the pictures.

Tutankhamun was showing them a magnificent set of hieroglyphic pictures, whose gold, white, blue, red, yellow and silver paintwork glistened in the light of their torches. At the top of each painting, seven silver stars shone out of a dark-blue background. Standing at the base of the pictures, was the stylised figure of a Pharaoh, bathed in a marvellous golden light, which seemed to streak out of the heavens. The whole design was surrounded by a seven-sided star shape.

'It's beautiful,' said Adam, and turned back to Tutankhamun. 'But what does it all mean?'

'Sukaru, Ak'Hara! Sukaru Ak'Hara! Amtoudi. Sukaru Amtoudi. Ak'Hara! Ak'Hara!'

Megabyte stepped forward towards the boy-king, but before he could reach him the image had faded from sight once again, leaving Adam and Megabyte with nothing but questions.

Amtoudi again. Who, or what, was Amtoudi? And what was its connection with the disappearance of Millicent and the missing Pharaoh, Rameses Ak'Hara.

Too many questions! Adam cursed. *And never enough answers!*

High in his secret tower, the man known as Sam Rees considered the images of Adam and Megabyte displayed in the centre of his glass pyramid. He fingered the pendant which hung about his neck and, as he did so, the diamond-shape at its centre began to glow.

A thousand memories, and a thousand different emotions were unlocked in his mind as he watched Adam and Megabyte in the tomb. There were happy memories, and recollections of unbearable sadness; faces he had known and almost loved down through the years, and faces for whom he only knew black and burning hate. Yet overriding them all was the knowledge of the task ahead of him.

Sam Rees stared deep into the pyramid, and the images of Adam and Megabyte faded, to be replaced by that of Ami. He smiled, a cruel, vicious smile.

'You have done well,' he told her. 'You have served me faithfully. But now it is time to bid farewell to all of you.'

Sam Rees closed his eyes, linking his mind to Ami's, adding his powers to her. Soon she and her infernal two friends would be no more, and then there would be no one left to stand in the way of Sam Rees' plans for domination over all sentient life in the entire universe.

Megabyte looked urgently at Adam. The ground was shaking beneath their feet, and a deep thrumming sound was coming from somewhere far off. He had a very bad feeling about all this . . .

The walls of the tomb started to vibrate, and slabs of rock dislodged themselves from the ceiling, narrowly missing them by inches. The thrumming noise had reached a terrible crescendo now and the floor started to buckle sickeningly beneath their feet, shaking them about like dice in a can. Megabyte clasped his stomach, willing himself not to throw up as the vibrations made his entire body shake. Half of the ceiling crashed down to the floor, sending up a throat-stinging cloud of white dust.

'The whole place is caving in!' Megabyte called out above the noise. 'Teleport!'

Megabyte felt Adam grab him by the arm, and pointed through the clouds of dust.

'Ami!'

Ami stood there, a little way off from them, seemingly oblivious of the devastation going on all around her. Her arms were outstretched, and there was a macabre smile on her face; around her neck Sam Rees' pendant blazed red and fiery.

Sam Rees had joined his mind with Ami, increasing her powers of telekinesis a thousand fold. Like an evil demon of destruction, Ami was using her psychic abilities to bring the whole pyramid tumbling down on her and friends.

Ami had come to the lost pyramid of Rameses Ak'Hara to bury them all alive.

Chapter Twelve

Ami looked curiously at the faces of Adam and Megabyte, as another chunk of masonry crashed to the ground. A crack opened up in the ground, and rapidly ran towards the furthermost wall. The sarcophagus tumbled off its dias and smashed to the floor.

Ignoring the destruction and havoc all around him, Adam raced over to Ami and grabbed her by the shoulders, and stared deep into her eyes. Ami looked back at him: she seemed to recognise him from somewhere a long, long time ago. And somehow she also realised that she was about to die: but that was what Sam Rees wanted, wasn't it, so it had to be.

'Ami!' Adam said, and shook her violently: Ami didn't resist. 'What's wrong with you? What are you doing here?'

'Get out of here!' Megabyte cried. 'The whole place is about to go!'

It was then that Adam saw the pendant around Ami's neck, its centre glowing with an uncanny fire. He reached out for it, and Ami shoved him away from her, spitting and snarling at him like an angry cat.

'Get your hands off it!' she hissed. 'Don't touch it, it's mine!' She reached up and cupped if protectively in her hands.

Megabyte looked at the crack along the floor, and up the wall. A huge fissure was opening up where the wall met the ceiling of the tomb.

'It's gonna go, Adam!'

Adam leapt on to Ami, and lunged for her pendant. Ami hit him with a strength Adam had never before suspected she possessed, and he fell back. Shaken he tried again, and this time managed to grab the leather thong to which the pendant was attached. With an almighty heave, he pulled the pendant from Ami's neck. Ami screamed out in pain.

'Get out now!' Megabyte cried and vanished in a flash of energy.

Adam looked up at the ceiling. He had less than a second to act. He grabbed hold of Ami and teleported them both away, as millions of tons of earth crashed down, burying the last tomb of Rameses Ak'Hara for all eternity.

'I wanted to kill you!' Ami said and buried her face in her hands and sobbed. 'And I nearly did! How can I say I'm sorry!'

Adam put a comforting arm around her shoulder.

All three of them had teleported back to the spaceship, where Ami had now been sleeping for several hours. When she had woken up the full horror of what she had done finally struck home, and no amount of comforting from Adam or Megabyte could console her.

'Ami, you don't have to apologise for anything,' Megabyte assured her, and Ami nodded her thanks. 'Do you remember anything? Apart from the bad feelings, that is?'

Ami thought hard, trying to resurrect memories which she wanted to bury forever. 'I just remember his eyes . . .' she said.

'Whose eyes?' Adam asked urgently, realising even now that they had no idea who their real enemy was.

'I don't know,' she admitted. 'But there were cold, burning, evil eyes. And then I remember being in a big and noisy city – I suppose it must have been Cairo – and following you somehow into that place . . .'

'We're up against someone who's got tremendous powers here,' Adam realised. 'Someone who can take possession of the mind of a Tomorrow Person, and make them go against their natural inability to kill . . .'

'But powers that have got limits!' Ami insisted. 'Otherwise we'd all have been dead long ago.'

'So where do we go from here?' Megabyte asked. 'Clue number one: an empty sarcophagus . . .'

'And here's clue number two,' Adam said, and took from out of his pocket the pendant he had ripped from Ami's neck. Ami winced, and turned away from the evil amulet.

Megabyte took the pendant from Adam, and examined it closely. He pointed out the star shape which had been etched on to its surface. 'I'm getting a real talent for noticing things,' he said smugly. 'Have you seen this shape someplace else before.'

'On the walls of the tomb,' Adam remembered. 'It was repeated all over the walls.'

'Could it be important?' Ami asked.

'There's only one way to find out,' Adam said. 'I bet Amanda James would be really interested in this!' He looked at Ami, his face full of concern. 'Are you up to teleporting back to London?' Ami nodded.

Megabyte stood up. 'While you see Amanda James I'm gonna do some homework of my home,' he told them. 'Tate and his freakshow friend will still be on their way back from Cairo, so Temple Hall will be empty. I'll go there, see what I can find out.'

'Be careful, Megabyte,' Ami said. 'We don't know what we're dealing with here . . .'

Adam took the pendant back from Megabyte and examined its mysterious star shape. 'But whatever it is, I can sense that time's running out . . .'

'Where did you kids get this?' Amanda James said in astonishment, as she held up to the light the pendant Adam and Ami had brought her.

'On a junk jewellery store,' Ami said. 'It was a birthday present.'

Amanda James turned angrily on the two Tomorrow People. 'Look, if you two are playing some sort of game with me here . . .'

'We're not,' Adam said, and the tone in his voice somehow reassured Amanda that they were indeed telling the truth.

'Does it mean something?' Ami asked. 'Please tell us.'

'This is a relic from way before the First Intermediate Period,' Amanda said. 'Somewhere, I estimate, between the sixth and seventh dynasties of the Old Kingdom.'

Adam pointed out the star shape on the pendant. 'We've seen that shape somewhere else – in a tomb . . .'

'What tomb?'

'We found a lost tomb in the western desert, near a place called Sa'ba,' Adam continued, blithely ignoring Amanda's incredulous look. 'The same pattern was repeated all over the place. We wondered if you know what it means . . .'

'There are no undiscovered tombs at Sa'ba,' Amanda stated categorically. 'I've been there.'

'If a tomb hasn't been discovered then how can you possibly say that it isn't there,' Adam asked quite reasonably.

This was too much for Amanda. 'Look, where did

you two really get this pendant from?' she asked. 'And exactly who are you?'

'It doesn't matter,' Ami said quickly. 'The important thing is that we need your help. What does the star shape mean?'

Nothing! One big fat zero! Megabyte said to himself. He had been at Temple Hall for an hour now, rifling through filing cabinets and upturning desk drawers to get at their contents, but so far he had come across nothing that might reveal the extent of Tate and Scully's plans, or indeed who their mysterious master might be.

In the upstairs rooms he had come across bookshelves creaking under the weight of old books about the paranormal and the occult: *mystical claptrap* he called it. There were also a surprisingly large amount of up-to-the-minute scientific textbooks, as well as several recent academic papers from the Royal Astronomical Society, in addition to the expected number of books on the history and religion of Ancient Egypt.

Megabyte was about to give up when he noticed a long cardboard tube, about eighteen inches long, perched on top of a filing cabinet. Hardly suspecting to find anything of interest he picked up the tube, and drew out its contents.

Sitting down at a desk, Megabyte unfurled a large astronomical photograph of a star system. It was similar to hundreds of others he had seen reproduced in magazines or the scientific journals his dad often brought home from work, and he thought nothing more of it. What did intrigue him, however, was Tate and Scully's apparent interest in the night sky. Somehow they didn't really strike Megabyte as being your typical astronomy buffs.

Megabyte was about to replace the photograph back inside its cardboard tube, when he noticed a formation of seven stars which shone much more brightly than the myriad others in the photograph. The pattern they formed in the night sky seemed strangely familiar . . .

With a beating heart Megabyte looked down at the bottom of the photograph, ignoring the masses of technical data printed there, and instead looking at the caption which identified the picture.

Star System Amtoudi. He had found Tutankhamun's mysterious Amtoudi at last!

Chapter Thirteen

Adam and Ami sat disconsolately on a park bench outside the museum, after having been summarily dismissed by Amanda James. She was a scientist, she had told them, accustomed to believing only the evidence of her own eyes. She was not someone prepared to believe cock-and-bull stories about long-lost tombs being discovered in the desert, tombs which were now no longer there because the roof had just conveniently caved in.

'Put yourself in her shoes,' Adam said philosophically. 'Two kids wander in off the street with a crazy story and expect you to believe it!'

'But it feels like we're so close to understanding!' Ami said, giving vent to her frustration. She looked up into the afternoon sky, as if that might give her some anser. 'What do we have to do now? Where do we go from here?'

'Evenin', all!'

Ami looked in the direction of the voice, and her eyes popped out of her head as she saw Red Rainwear, Lizzie Motherwell, and Rupert Short, who she recognised from Adam's description. They were sitting on an adjacent bench – a bench that just a second ago had been empty. All three of them were eating popcorn from enormous cardboard tubs, and Red Rainwear's umbrella was up, even though it wasn't raining. Come to think of it, Ami realised, in spite of Red Rainwear's greeting it wasn't even late afternoon yet.

Red Rainwear shook hands with Adam, 'We hear you've had some lovely luck,' the little man grinned.

'Er, some,' Adam admitted. 'But how do you guys know?'

'Gossip!' came the answer. 'Like raspberry jam and lemon curd, it spreads! You found the tomb?'

Adam nodded, and Red Rainwear turned to his two friends and gave a little whoop of triumph. Lizzie and Rupert burst into a round of spontaneous applause, but, as usual, didn't say a word.

For the first time Red Rainwear noticed Ami who was staring agog at the three surreal characters Adam and Megabyte had told her about. He brought a hand to his mouth, and clucked shamefully.

'Please forgive our atrocious manners!' he said. 'You, of course, must be Ami.'

'That's right.'

Red Rainwear looked up at Ami for a second, and frowned, as if he was about to ask a terribly serious question. 'Is that Ami with an "i"?'

'Yes.'

'And not Ami with a "y"?'

'No.'

Red Rainwear screeched with laughter. '"Y" not?' he asked, and beside him Lizzie and Rupert broke into convulsions of mirth.

Ami glanced at Adam, begging him to free her from the three weirdos, Adam smiled helplessly and introduced them to her as friends of Millicent.

'Have you any news of her?' Ami asked Red Rainwear.

At the mention of Millicent's name, Red Rainwear and his two colleagues abruptly stopped laughing. Their jolly smiling faces now took on the demeanour of guests at a funeral.

'We were rather hoping that you might have some,' Red Rainwear admitted mournfully. 'Mrs Motherwell's had a funny twinge in her left leg since last night, haven't you, Mrs Motherwell?' Lizzie Motherwell nodded sadly and raised her voluminous skirt to reveal a surprisingly shapely leg which she started to rub. 'And Mrs Motherwell's leg is as reliable as Big Ben,' Red Rainwear continued. 'It can mean only one thing: Millicent's in terrible danger. We might already be too late: you have to hurry!'

'We've tried everything,' Adam despaired, 'but we're just going round in circles. We found the Zuzu Club and the Cartouche, we found the tomb. But nobody's interested in anything except what they can see. And apart from this – ' he held up the pendant – 'we haven't got a thing!'

'But you discovered the tomb,' Red Rainwear protested. 'You must have found the answer!'

'All we found was an empty sarcophagus and some paintings on the wall.' Adam said, 'But now they're all destroyed.'

'Gone but not forgotten,' Red Rainwear said with a sudden twinkle in his eye. He glanced over at Rupert, who took several large sheets of cartridge paper from out of his school satchel, which he handed to Red Rainwear who, in turn, gave them to Adam. Mrs Motherwell took a set of colour felt-tip pens out of her apron pocket and passed them over to Adam, giggling with embarrassment as she did so.

Adam looked blankly at the paper and pens. 'What am I supposed to do with these?' he asked, but it was Ami who realised what Red Rainwear was suggesting.

'The tomb paintings, Adam!'

Red Rainwear clapped his hands with glee. 'Clever girl! Did you get a good look at them, Adam? Can you remember them?'

'Yes, but so what? Hang on, you mean . . .'

'Attaboy!' cheered the little man. 'Now we're getting places! Now we're cooking with gas!'

Grinning, Adam started to draw.

'I have never seen anything like this before in my life,' Amanda James gasped, after Adam and Ami had returned to her office with eight sheets of A3 cartridge paper covered with the designs Adam had seen painted on the tomb wall. They were all tacked up, side by side, on Amanda's office wall now, a near-perfect life-sized reproduction of the paintings from the tomb of Rameses Ak'Hara.

'Of course it's only rough,' Adam said modestly, and pinned the ninth sheet onto the wall. He had drawn this sheet right here in Amanda's office with the Egyptologist watching on in amazement. 'But it gives you the general idea . . .'

'You did all this from memory?' Amanda said incredulously. 'It's unbelievable.'

'It doesn't mean it's not real though, does it?' Ami asked pointedly.

'OK, I believe you,' Amanda said at long last, and Adam and Ami grinned. 'What is it you want to know?'

'What does it mean?' Adam asked, and pointed to the illustration he had copied from the tomb: the seven silver stars shining in a cobalt-blue background, and the figure of a Pharaoh, standing in a shaft of golden light.

Amanda considered the painting carefully, examining each section of it in detail. She stroked her chin thoughtfully, went to her bookshelf to check up on a few references, and then returned to the painting with a large reference book.

'How's your history?' she asked, after a pause of about five minutes.

'Not so hot,' Ami admitted candidly.

'History's a lot more relevant than you might think,' Amanda said, and opened her book to a photograph of a monument which was familiar to both Adam and Ami: the Great Pyramid of Cheops. 'It took thirty years to build that and two and a half million perfectly engineered blocks of stone. Some of those blocks weighed as much as fifteen tons . . .'

Adam could see what Amanda was hinting at. 'And the Ancient Egyptians did all that with no cranes, no heavy lifting gear . . .'

'The truth is that we still don't know how they did it, just as there are so many things we don't understand about life in Ancient Egypt,' Amanda admitted. 'But they were people – just like you or me – and there's bound to be a scientific answer.'

'But they did worship the stars, didn't they?' Adam asked.

'They lived by them; the stars ruled their whole lives. You can see it everywhere in all the ancient hieroglyphs.' She considered the reconstructed tomb painting, and pointed out the configuration of stars on it. 'But I've never seen anything quite like this before . . .'

Adam indicated the golden light streaking out of the sky on to the Pharoah. 'And what's this?'

Amanda hesitated for a moment, and then went over to her book shelf to consult an old leather-bound book. 'There's a myth – and it's only a myth –

that during the time of the Old Kingdom, around 2600BC, there was a cult of mystics obsessed with the idea that the stars in the sky could give them phenomenal powers of magic. The story goes that they used their powers to build the Pyramids.' She looked at Adam and Ami's faces: they were clearly drinking in every word. 'Of course, it's only a story,' she reminded them. 'A myth, a legend, nothing more!'

'Who exactly were these mystics?' Adam asked urgently. 'Did they have a leader . . . Was it Rameses Ak'Hara?'

Amanda was stunned at Adam's knowledge, as pieces of the jigsaw slowly fell into place. These kids were telling the truth after all! 'Yes . . .' she said weakly.

'It was his tomb!' Adam said, and pointed back at the paintings on the wall. 'Those hieroglyphs came from the tomb of Rameses Ak'Hara! He wasn't a myth: he was real!'

'It's madness . . .' Amanda said.

Ami pointed at the familiar seven-sided star shape which was repeated everywhere on the tomb painting. She demanded to know what it signified, Amanda stared at the painting for long minutes, and then took one of Adam's felt-tip pens from off the desk. She stepped up to the drawing and started to join up several of the largest stars in the design, as if she was completing a huge join-the-dots puzzle.

When she had finished she gave Adam and Ami a triumphant look: the seven stars formed the familiar larger star shape.

'It's the shape of the stars!' Adam realised.

'It's a symbolic representation of Amtoudi,' Amanda explained and was taken aback by the excited looks on Adam and Ami's faces.

'Amtoudi!' Ami gasped, remembering the words of Tutankhamun. 'What is Amtoudi?'

'It's a star system in the northern sky,' Amanda told them, and then hesitated before continuing: 'Amtoudi was also the name of the mystics – because those were the very seven stars they worshipped.'

'Seven stars, seven pyramids,' Ami said. 'Adam there has to be a connection!'

'We need to know more,' Adam said. 'What else does the story say?'

Amanda consulted her reference book again. 'That Rameses Ak'Hara was a tyrant who misused his powers for evil. And that he was made immortal by a heavenly light . . .'

All three of them turned to the picture of the Pharaoh bathing in the golden light.

'Amanda, what else do the old stories tell us?' Ami asked.

'Nothing,' she replied, and slammed the book closed. 'As I said, it's just a myth. Almost every single hieroglyph that mentions the story was vandalised at some time in history.'

'Why?'

Amanda shrugged. 'One tyrant comes along, topples everything, and forces a new order on what went before. That's the way that history works: sometimes things that matter most get destroyed.'

Or else people destroy things to prevent other people finding out their secrets, Adam suddenly realised. When Amanda crossed over to the bookshelf to return her book, Adam looked at Ami.

'Those hieroglyphs were deliberately destroyed,' he told her with certainty. 'Just like the Rameses Cartouche was meant to be destroyed.'

'Adam, what are you saying?'

'Rameses Ak'Hara faked his death; that's why we found an empty sarcophagus. He faked his burial, faked the whole darn thing. And he's still alive!'

'It's what Millicent said,' Ami suddenly realised, and recalled the old woman's words, '"The stone shall move, the stars will shine, a shadow long shall fall upon the Earth".' She shivered. 'Adam, I'm scared, I'm really scared . . .'

Chapter Fourteen

– Now you guys are just not going to believe the stuff that I have found out! Megabyte's voice rang out loud and clear in Adam and Ami's mind.

– Me and Ami have discovered something unbelievably mind-blowing!

Megabyte wasn't impressed by Adam's boast. *– Oh yeah? Well, I bet you it's not as unbelievably mind-blowing as my discovery!*

– Bet it is!

– Bet it isn't!

The two guys' mental bickering would have continued for hours if Ami hadn't done the sensible thing and punched Adam in the ribs. She and Adam homed in on Megabyte's brainwaves and teleported to his side – but not to where they expected.

'This isn't Temple Hall,' Adam said, and looked around the laboratory where Megabyte was working at a desk, arms-deep in files and papers. Several pieces of futuristic pieces of equipment were dotted around the room.

Megabyte looked up. 'It's part of the Royal Observatory in Greenwich: some new annex, I guess,' he told them. He stood up and regarded his two friends smugly. 'Well, do you want to blow my mind – or shall I blow yours?'

'Amtoudi's a star system!' all three of them said in unison.

Somewhat deflated, Megabyte showed Adam and Ami the rolled-up photograph of Amtoudi. 'I found this at Tate's place,' he said.

'So what are you doing here now?' Ami asked.

'Amtoudi was photographed from here,' Megabyte said, and turned the black and white over. On the back had been printed the words: *With compliments Felix Fry, Greenwich Observatory*. 'That's what led me here, together with all this stuff down the side.' Megabyte showed them the series of computer-generated figures running down the side of the photograph. 'Times, dates and angles . . .'

Ami picked up the photograph. 'That's today's date!' she suddenly realised.

'I know,' said Megabyte. 'So I got to thinking why would anybody need all this kind of information?' He picked up an armload of files and led them away from the desk and to a more open part of the laboratory. 'You think that's interesting? Boy, are you ever in for a big surprise!'

Tate and a middle-aged, dour-looking man dressed in

a long white coat strolled up the hill leading to Greenwich Observatory. In the distance the tallest skyscraper in London gleamed in the light of the sun, looking like a modern hi-tech version of Cleopatra's Needle.

'Have the final checks all been attended to, Mister Fry?' Tate asked his companion, and Fry nodded.

'Everything's ready to roll!' he said, scarcely able to contain the excitement in his voice.

'Excellent!' Tate approved. 'We have come a long way in the past ten years, Mister Fry. Your contribution has been of fundamental importance to this project.'

'I'm just so grateful that you chose me to be involved in such a fantastic piece of science!'

'Mister Rees has asked me to convey his appreciation to you for all you have done.'

Fry acknowledged the thanks and then rubbed his hands with glee. 'I just can't wait for tonight,' he said. 'It's going to be like heaven on Earth!'

'We shall see,' Tate said and chuckled at Fry's unintended irony. He stopped at the entrance to the observatory and made his farewells to the scientist. 'It is possible that you may quite soon be receiving a delegation of three young people . . .'

'Scientists?'

'Scientists,' Tate confirmed and continued casually: 'If they do appear I suggest that you at once redirect them to Mister Rees. He is most anxious that they understand . . . everything . . .'

At the far end of Fry's lab there was a large bench on which had been placed a small model pyramid, about nine inches high. The pyramid had been surrounded by several pieces of electrical gadgetery, the purpose of which none of them could guess. Overhead, several stubby tubes were positioned in the ceiling, directly over the pyramid; they reminded Adam of light projectors.

Megabyte led Adam and Ami to a control console a little way off from the experimental apparatus, and dumped his load of files there.

'This is weird,' Ami said, as she stopped by the bench and bent down to look at the pyramid: it seemed to be constructed of a strange crystalline substance she had never seen before.

'That's what I thought at first,' Megabyte said, and opened up one of the files. He checked a few lines of instructions contained inside, and then flicked a switch on the control console: the machine buzzed into life. 'I've spent the last couple of hours going through these notes trying to make sense of it. And then I came across this file: *Top secret – do not read*, it said, the sort of thing I can't resist. Guys, you are not going to believe this.'

He called Ami away from the pyramid, and initiated a sequence of commands on the control console, all the time referring to the notes in the top-secret file. The electronic apparatus around the pyramid started to crackle with energy.

'Our Mister Fry's been doing some real serious research into energy in his laboratory,' Megabyte said, as he checked an on-screen computer read-out.

'You mean, nuclear power?' Ami asked, but Megabyte shook his head.

'No *natural* energy, the clean kind with no pollution at all.'

'Wind power . . . waves?' Adam asked. 'What's all this got to do with astronomy?'

'Forget wind and waves, Adam,' Megabyte said. 'This is astrophysics!' He hit a button and the light projectors above the pyramid whirred into life; they started to flow faintly. 'This is pyramid power!' he announced grandly.

'Pyramid power?' Adam had no idea what Megabyte was talking about.

Megabyte pointed to the model pyramid on the bench. 'It's the shape, Adam; that's the clue. The theory is that, in nature, every shape carries with it its own energy field. For instance, the natural energy of a circle would be different to the energy of a square. With me so far?'

Adam and Ami nodded.

'And there's something very special about the shape of a pyramid,' Megabyte continued, and adjusted a control. The light projectors began to blaze now with an unearthly brilliance. 'Did you know that if you put a piece of cheese inside a pyramid-shaped box it stays fresh longer than if you put it into a round one? And that if you put a blunt razor inside the same box it will sharpen? That's just a tiny part of what pyramid power can do.'

'The Ancient Egyptians must have known about that,' Adam said.

'Science has known about energy-within-shapes forever,' Megabyte said airily. 'But so what? Shapes carry energy, big deal. How do you get to it? How do you unlock that power?'

'Someone's found a way?' Adam asked, and Megabyte nodded furiously.

'This Felix Fry guy has – and it's so simple. It's light, that's all it is! Now watch this, guys!' Megabyte hit a button, and the light projectors beamed down on to the pyramid.

For a second the pyramid was surrounded by several shafts of blazing laser-light, and then the shafts reformed themselves, joining together to produce a pyramid of light which hovered directly above the solid pyramid.

'It's the big breakthrough everyone's been waiting for!' Megabyte said. 'All you have to do is to shine a special frequency light source, focused into the exact same shape of the object, then match the two together – '

Megabyte adjusted a further control, and slowly the light pyramid floated down and wrapped itself around the model pyramid, fitting into its contours like a hand slipping into a glove.

'And hey presto, it releases all the natural energy.'

There was a blinding flash of light so dazzling that Adam, Ami and Megabyte were forced to shield their eyes. Quarks, and anti-quarks, tau-mesons and tauons, protons and neutrons all danced around the pyramid, creating an amazing limitless fountain of energy.

'The energy creates the light and the light creates the energy!' Megabyte shouted. 'A free source of energy for everyone!' He closed down the machine and the pyramid of energy vanished.

'All that force and power from nowhere, it's phenomenal,' said Adam when he had time to catch his breath.

'And that was just a tiny model,' Ami realised, and walked over to the model pyramid. It wasn't even hot.

'Can you imagine the amount of energy you could let fly from a full-sized pyramid?' Megabyte asked.

'It could revolutionise everything,' Ami said. 'Endless fire and natural energy, with no pollution . . .'

'It could save our planet,' Adam agreed. 'Or destroy it.'

'Good afternoon. Step right into my laboratory, why don't you?'

The three TPs turned around to see Fry standing there, an amused look on his face. He saw that Megabyte had been reading his top-secret files. 'A good read, was it?' Megabyte mumbled an apology he didn't mean.

'You really shouldn't have broken into my laboratory, you know,' Fry said and started to collect up the papers Megabyte had been reading. 'This is all private research.'

'Whose private research?' Ami wanted to know.

'The Rees Foundation,' Fry answered. 'Sam Rees's company.'

'What's *his* angle on all this?' Megabyte asked. The name rang a vague bell with him: some big-time industrialist, he recalled: didn't he own that big skyscraper down by the docks? 'What's in it for Sam Rees?'

Fry tut-tutted like an old uncle reprimanding a recalcitrant nephew. 'That's a very cynical question, young man,' he reproved. 'Not everyone who lends support to research has an angle. There are people who happen to believe that science is of some value to the world.'

'But a discovery like this brings with it some responsibilities,' Adam pointed out. 'If it gets into the wrong hands . . .'

Always supposing it's not in the wrong hands already, he added to himself.

'That's not my concern,' Fry said. 'That's what the men in suits are for!'

'But it does matter what Sam Rees does with this power!' Ami said. 'I can't believe you don't care.'

'I am a scientist with work to do,' Fry told her. 'Mister Rees's money means that I can push forward the boundaries of science. That's what matters – creating the occasional revolution.'

'What are you guys up to anyway?' Adam asked, and Fry merely chuckled and handed him a business card.

'Why not ask him yourself?' he said. 'Apparently he's expecting you . . .'

Chapter Fifteen

With a sinking heart, Adam looked up at the imposing facade of the Rees Foundation building. Its angled roof, red in the light of the sun, reminded him of a pyramid, and for the first time he was struck by the resemblance of the tallest skyscraper in London to Cleopatra's Needle down on the Thames. With his every nerve alert for danger Adam entered the building.

The reception hall, constructed out of sleek black marble, was empty. No reception clerk, no security guards, no harrassed office workers rushing from meeting to meeting. It was as dead as the grave – or the lost tomb of Rameses Ak'Hara in the distant Egyptian deserts.

Or not quite. As Adam strode purposefully across the hall, his feet echoing noisily on the cold marble floor, one pair of eyes watched his every move. Rees's cat has spotted Adam, and licked its lips in anticipation of the final feast that would soon be its.

There was a bank of elevators at the far end of the

hall and as Adam approached one, its doors whispered open for him. Taking a deep breath, Adam stepped into it, and the doors closed behind him. The elevator began to ascend to the very top of the building.

For some reason, the phrase *Walking straight into the lion's den* came into Adam's mind.

'Are you sure Adam's going to be OK?' Ami asked, as she and Megabyte walked into the reading room of the British library; there was still several hours to go before it closed for the day.

'He'll be fine,' Megabyte reassured her. When they had received Sam Rees' 'invitation', Adam had decided that he should go alone; as he had said, there was no sense in all three of them walking into what was so obviously a trap. 'Nobody teleports out of trouble faster than Adam! But what are we doing here?'

'I've remembered something Millicent said just before she was bundled away into that car,' Ami said and handed a Request Form to the librarian. 'Something about reading the papers. I think I've just worked out what she meant!'

'So what are we looking for?' Megabyte asked, as the librarian went off to bring the items Ami had asked for.

'The newspapers of course!'

'Silly of me not to realise,' Megabyte said. 'The

world could be coming to an end and we're looking at newspapers!'

'Not just any newspapers,' Ami said irritably, as the librarian returned with a pile of yellowing old newspapers, and a box full of newspaper clippings and old photographs, 'Newspapers from 1878.'

'I see,' said Megabyte, not seeing at all.

'The year Cleopatra's Needle was brought to England, of course!' Ami said, and led Megabyte over to an unoccupied desk. 'It kept coming back to my mind: Cleopatra's Needle, the warning from Tutankhamun. It was all so much tied up with Cleopatra's Needle but I couldn't see why it was so important. So then I got to thinking – how did it come to be taken away from Egypt and brought to London in the first place? Now let's get looking!'

'For what?'

Ami shrugged. 'I guess we'll know what we're looking for when we find it!'

Megabyte sighed and started to rifle through the box of press cuttings and photos. He picked one out, and read it aloud. 'Seventeenth September 1878 . . . great Egyptian monument unveiled . . . blah-blah-blah . . . for the greater glory of our beloved Queen Victoria . . .'

'That's just waffle,' Ami said. 'Look at the photographs . . .'

Megabyte took one of the sepia-tinted photographs and peered at it. It showed a group of

Victorian businessmen, dressed in top hats and frock coats, standing at the base of Cleopatra's Needle. 'These must be the guys who brought the Needle back from Egypt, right?'

Ami nodded, and returned to reading an old copy of *The Times* from that date. Suddenly Megabyte grabbed her arm, and pointed to the photograph, at the bottom of which had been written the names of all the men present at the monument's inauguration.

'Oswald, Huntley . . . *and Rees!*

Ami indicated a brief report in *The Times*. 'Wealthy City industrialist, Mister Samuel Rees, whose firm, the Rees Coal and Gas Company, financed the operation . . .' she read out.

'You mean the Sam Rees in that picture and in that article are somehow related to the Sam Rees that Adam's going to see?'

'Not related, Megabyte,' Ami said darkly.

'You can't be serious,' Megabyte said, but the worried look on Ami's face proved that she was.

'It's impossible,' Megabyte protested. 'Ami, that picture's a hundred and twenty years old. It's just not possible!'

But in both their hearts they knew that it was true. The Sam Rees waiting for Adam in his tower, and the Samuel Rees who had shipped Cleopatra's Needle over to England at the height of the Victorian age, were one and the same person.

Finally, after what seemed an eternity to Adam but

was in reality a little less than half a minute, the elevator came to a halt and the doors glided open. Adam swallowed hard and, with a trembling heart, stepped into the sanctum sanctorum of the man he had come to know as Sam Rees.

The room was cavernous and cold, and in the semi-darkness – the only light came from four flaming braziers placed at each of the four cardinal points – Adam could see that each of the towering walls was covered with Egyptian hieroglyphics, hewn into the wall. On the far wall was suspended a huge Egyptian bird, its mighty turquoise and golden winds outstretched to sweep up the entire world. In one of its claws, burning with an eerie purple light, was the Marhaba Stone.

Before the bird, Sam Rees sat at his ebony desk, gazing into the glass pyramid. On a side desk Adam saw the great model city that he had seen at Temple Hall: Sam Rees's plans for his new seat of power when he took over the world. When Rees became aware of Adam's presence, he stood up and moved to the front of his desk to greet him.

'You are most welcome.'

Rees's voice made Adam's blood freeze, but he resolved not to let the man know how scared and intimidated he really was. He showed Adam to a chair by the side of his desk. Adam sat down and Rees resumed his place on the other side of the desk. Neither of them took their eyes off each other.

'You're Rameses Ak'Hara, aren't you?' Adam said, and Rees acknowledged the fact with an almost imperceptible nod of his head.

'Sam Rees – Rameses,' Adam said and chuckled ironically. 'A cute anagram.'

'Where are the others?' Rees demanded.

'So you can kill us all in one fell swoop?' Adam asked, 'Do you think we're really that stupid?'

'It is apparent that you are not,' Rees said. 'But I repeat my question: where are they?'

'Around,' Adam replied defiantly.

The man known as Sam Rees and who had once been Rameses Ak'Hara, tyrant Pharaoh of all Egypt, regarded Adam through soulless and all-appraising eyes. 'The boy Tutankhamun was one of your kind,' he said finally and registered Adam's startled reaction. 'Oh yes, I know all about your kind, all about the so-called Tomorrow People. You and your friends are not the first, I have encountered others of you on my long journey down the centuries.'

'Tutankhamun was one of the first Tomorrow People – maybe even the very first one,' Adam said. 'You knew him?'

'Of course. He rose to become Pharaoh of my homeland, some considerable time after my own ascension. He was a fine boy – but interfering, like you and your friends.'

'You killed him!' Adam suddenly realised. He remembered his old history lessons, how the boy-king had died suddenly at the age of eighteen and how many historians believed that he had been murdered.

'It was necessary.' There was no emotion in Rees' voice, no trace of sorrow or regret. 'Just as killing you is necessary. The emergence of you and your kind on this planet is anathema to me. You are freaks of nature that must be crushed. I have killed your kind before; I shall kill them again.'

'Then you're insane,' Adam said. 'Tomorrow People are breaking out all over the world right this minute. Humankind is evolving, moving forward, getting better. Evolution is not something that you can stop!'

'You live in a pitiful dreamworld,' Rees sneered. 'What do you see when you look around you? Nothing but chaos and anarchy, and a complete collapse of order. And it is I, the immortal Rameses Ak'Hara who shall restore order to this Earth.'

'You're not the first person to think like that!' Adam said. 'And like them you'll never succeed. You can't play around with the laws of the universe. We live; we die. Those are the rules.'

'They are not my rules,' Rees said. 'I am Rameses Ak'Hara and with the power of the Marhaba Stone and the Pyramids I can do what I choose.' He rose from his chair, and looked down on Adam as he would an insect. 'I shall live forever and reign supreme over all people.'

Never, was what Adam's look of contempt seemed to say. He stood up to face Rees.

'You'll fail!' he told him. 'You're doomed to fail.'

'And you are doomed to die.

Adam tried to teleport himself away, and found to his horror that he couldn't. He looked at Rees with wild, and frightened eyes; Rees's own eyes blazed red with malign power.

Realising that Rees was somehow negating his own psychic powers, Adam turned and ran for the elevator door. He froze to a halt; it was no longer there, dissolved into the ebony of the walls by the power of Rees's own mind. This was Sam Rees's own domain, Adam realised with terror, and here all natural laws were suspended and bent to his own will.

'Goodbye, accursed one, goodbye for ever,' said Sam Rees. Bolts of energy burst from his eyes, and enveloped Adam in the same mists which had earlier so effectively disposed of Millicent F. Rutherford.

The mists penetrated into every fibre of Adam's being, stinging him, wracking his body with pain beyond imaginings. Adam suppressed a desire to scream out in torment, resolving that even in death he would not give Sam Rees that one final pleasure.

And then Adam was gone, obliterated from the face of the Earth, for all eternity.

Chapter Sixteen

'Something's happened to Adam – he's been away far too long,' Megabyte said. He and Ami had teleported back to the spaceship, where they were now going through photocopies of the newspaper articles they had tracked down.

'He knows what he's doing,' Ami said confidently, her concern for her friend tempered by the excitement of discovery. She knew she was on to something here: the newspaper articles could be another clue to the real plans of Sam Rees. She tossed a sheaf of old photographs over to Megabyte: Sam Rees was in every one of them, standing in front of Cleopatra's Needle.

Or at least that was what Ami thought until she sorted through some of the photocopies she had taken. Her eyes widened with disbelief, and she pointed them out to Megabyte.

'There wasn't just one obelisk, there were loads of them!' She read further, 'And they were all exactly like Cleopatra's Needle . . .'

'C'mon, give us a break . . .'

'No, it's true,' she said excitedly, and drew his attention to the article she was reading from *The Times*. 'And in the past two centuries they've all been moved and into cities all over Europe. In London, in Paris, in Rome . . . Sam Rees has spent the last two hundred years moving the obelisks over Europe like giant chess pieces!'

'This is important: we have to tell Adam,' Megabyte said, and closed his eyes to communicate with Adam. – *Adam? Adam?*

Silence. Even when Adam chose not to respond to Megabyte's telepathic messages, Megabyte was still always able to sense his best friend's presence, but now there was nothing. He looked anxiously at Ami who tried to contact him too: still silence.

'He's in big trouble,' Megabyte said.

'But he'd call us if he was, wouldn't he?' Ami said, and laid down the papers, as a cold feeling of dread passed over her. 'He'd teleport back to us.'

'I'm getting a sick, dark feeling,' Megabyte said, and shuddered. 'It's like he's been taken away from us, abandoned someplace evil . . .'

Ami's eyes shone with understanding. 'You're right! He's lost *between* places . . .'

'We've got to help him get away from there,' Megabyte said, and reached out for Ami's hands. If they mind-merged, allied their telepathic powers to each other's, then there might just be a chance. 'If together we can contact the past then maybe we can reach Adam – wherever he is . . .'

As they prepared themselves, neither Megabyte or Ami dared consider the other possibility. If Adam was not trapped in some limbo, some strange dimension between the here and the here, and the now and the now, then there was only one other alternative.

He was dead.

Is this death? Adam wondered as the mists cleared and he picked himself up off the mildewed stony floor, and looked around.

He was no longer in Sam Rees' sanctuary, but had been transported to some other place, a dark, ominous Gothic dungeon, whose stone walls shimmered and shifted as he tried to focus on them. The place was in darkness, a sort of sticky red darkness that reminded Adam of blood, and the air was vile and rank, making Adam want to gag. The place was a charnel house: skeletons, some still clothed in rags, lined the walls and littered the floor.

Every one of Adam's muscles was aching, but nevertheless he tried to stand up. No sooner had he dragged himself to his feet, than his head went woozy, the world started to spin around him, and he clattered back down to the stone floor.

From somewhere far off he could hear the sound of laughter, a cruel, vicious, mocking sound; and then that faded to be replaced by a hideous cawing noise, like the call of some giant hungry bird of prey. Much closer, he could hear a chorus of weeping and wailing, like the sound of the souls of the damned crying out in their never-ending torment. If there was a hell, Adam decided, then this was surely it.

Adam dragged himself across the floor, towards a stone bench, when suddenly, as if from out of nowhere, a hand gripped his shoulder. He turned, prepared to defend himself againt his attacker with whatever little strength he had left.

Millicent F. Rutherford collapsed into his arms, moaning softly. Her lips were cracked and swollen, her once-smiling face now a mask of abject terror and suffering, and her clothes were in rags.

'Millicent, you're alive!' Adam said, and held the old woman close to him; but not too tightly, for her body felt weak and fragile in his arms, as if it might crack at any second.

'Tonight . . . tonight . . .' Millicent muttered, half to herself. 'Too late . . .'

Using all his strength, Adam managed to help Millicent into a sitting position, resting her against the side of the stone bench. 'You're going to be fine,' he reassured her, and hoped he sounded convincing, but Millicent shook her head.

'The stars shine tonight,' she moaned.

'Save your strength,' Adam whispered. 'Let's see if I can get us out of this place.'

He slammed his eyes shut, summoning up all his

psychic energies for one final jaunt out of whatever hell he and Millicent had found themselves in. A few sparks of blue energy crackled around his body but that was all; Sam Rees' power stretched even to this dead-man's zone. He looked at the skeletons: were these also Tomorrow People, he wondered, who had dared to defy Rees in the past? Was this to be his fate as well?

No! he cried out with every fibre of his being. He was one of the Tomorrow People, part of the future of humankind. He could not allow Sam Rees' evil to run unchecked on the Earth and taint that future. And if he couldn't escape from here by himself, then he would have to ask the help of others.

– Ami? Megabyte? Can you hear me?

No reply. Only silence, save for that vicious mocking laugh from far away. Adam was alone.

He tried again. And again, focusing his every thought on to his friends, and the spaceship. By his side Millicent groaned: she wasn't going to hold out much longer, he guessed.

Nothing again.

No! There was something! A faint whispering in is ears, as though someone was trying to contact him.

– Adam . . . Adam . . .

– Guys! Get me out of here! Get me out now!

Nothing happened for long seconds. And then, as Ami and Megabyte and the spaceship merged their psychic powers with Adam's, Adam and Millicent were surrounded by a blue haze. Flickers of energy started to crack and spit around them, and Adam and Millicent slowly started to fade from view.

And then they became solid again. They were in Sam Rees' world now and he wasn't going to let them go without a struggle.

– *Come on, guys! Concentrate! Focus!*

Adam's head was ready to burst now, and sweat was pouring down his face. With one final effort he linked himself with his fellow Tomorrow People and their spaceship.

There was an enormous explosion of psychic energy, and Adam and Millicent were no more, leaving Sam Rees' world once more to the souls of the damned.

Chapter Seventeen

Adam looked on in concern as Megabyte and Ami helped to lay the almost unconscious Millicent next to the central core of the spaceship. Having been a prisoner of Sam Rees for so long, it seemed touch and go whether she would survive.

'What in heaven's name happened?' Ami asked.

Not in heavens *name*, Adam thought.

'We were both sent to some place to die,' he said. 'Only it wasn't a place: it was like somewhere imagined, outside of time, dreamed up in his mind.' He looked at Megabyte. 'You remember Millicent's "houseboat"? Well, this was like the exact opposite of that: a horrible killing field. And there were so many others, maybe other Tomorrow People. Dead, poor souls who've crossed Rees in the past.'

'Ak'Hara! The Evil One!'

They all rushed over to Millicent. Her body seemed suddenly to have recovered its lost strength; there was a vigour in her once again, as though she had somehow drawn energy and life from the spaceship's central core.

'A shadow long shall fall upon the Earth!' Millicent said.

'What does it all mean, Adam?' asked Megabyte. 'What's it all about, for crying out loud?'

'It's about power and the lust for power on a scale we can't even begin to imagine,' Adam said darkly. 'He wants nothing less than to rule the cosmos. And it happens tonight!'

'What happens tonight!' Ami asked.

'What Red Rainwear said,' Megabyte reminded her. 'Something monumental.'

'But what is it?' Adam wondered. 'If we're to stop it we need to know what it is!'

'Millicent, help us!' Ami pleaded. 'Time's running out! What do we do? Where do we go?'

'Take me home,' Millicent recited, in a strange and faraway voice. "Take me home, she weeps and wails" . . . we have to stop him tonight!'

Sam Rees looked down at the figure of Tate with contempt. Tate was a snivelling, ineffectual wretch who could still, however, serve Sam Rees' great purpose.

'From the beginning you have underestimated their powers,' he stated coldly.

'Me, my lord? I assure you . . .'

'Silence!' Sam Rees commanded. 'It is beyond the bounds of belief that my forty centuries of faultless planning can be endangered at this fateful, final hour. I hold you responsible.'

Tate bowed his head in shame and fear; he knew that Sam Rees was right. 'They had defied us for too long, mighty Rameses,' he admitted. 'What must be done to rid us of these wretched creatures?'

'I sense that even now the Forces of Light are assembling themselves to do battle,' Sam Rees said, making sure that his minion could not detect in his voice the apprehension he was feeling. 'We must acknowledge that they are not without potency. We must strive to know their minds, think their thoughts. If we do this we can – we must – outwit them.'

'As ever, my Lord, you are right,' Tate said, and raised his head, daring to look into the eyes of the great Sam Rees. Was his life going to be spared after all?

'By outwitting our enemies we destroy them. By destroying them we deliver ourselves from all menace. Then conquest will be mine – tonight!'

Sam Rees raised his arms heavenwards, as if he wanted to grasp and pull down the very firmament of stars itself. Above him, the Marhaba Stone glinted purple in the semi-darkness, preparing itself for the victory to come . . . 'You two do realise that this is complete and utter lunacy?' Megabyte said as he, Adam and Ami ran up the hill leading to Greenwich Observatory. Night was falling now, and in the distance the Rees Foundation Tower shone on the banks of the Thames, like a giant lightning conductor, pointing to heaven.

'Felix Fry is our only hope,' Ami reminded him. 'he's the only one who really knows what's going on.'

'And you actually think he's going to tell us the whole story in graphic detail?' Megabyte mocked. 'Get real! Let's get away from here before we get ourselves killed!'

They heard the crunching sound of footsteps on the gravel path, and turned. Felix Fry was running after them, an anxious look on his drawn and tired face.

'Am I glad to see you three!' Fry panted, when he had caught up with them. 'I hoped you'd come back! I've been a blessed fool!'

Adam, Ami and Megabyte exchanged puzzled looks: was this for real?

'We are very un-pleased with you, Mister Felix Fry.' Megabyte glowered at him. 'All that "go and ask Sam Rees" baloney; you set us up. You nearly got Adam here killed!'

'I didn't realise he planned to kill you,' Fry claimed, and ignored Adam's look of disbelief. 'We haven't got much time. Come with me; I'm going to tell you everything I know about this thing!'

As Fry led Adam, Ami and Megabyte into the Observatory, he told them that he had just eavesdropped on a private conversation between Rees and Tate. It was then that he'd realised he'd been deceived from the start: Rees had told him that all his researches into pyramid power were to be for the benefit of mankind; it was only now that he realised the true nature of Rees' ambitions.

'All right, we're listening,' Adam said, prepared to give the scientist the benefit of the doubt, at least for the moment.

Fry led the three of them into a darkened laboratory, about twice the size of the original one. In the centre of the room there stood a bank of computers and monitor screens, and a control console, similar to the one Megabyte had used earlier to demonstrate the power of the pyramid; laser-light projectors hung from the ceiling. Fry went up to the console and operated a control, bathing the entire room in light.

The floor on which the Tomorrow People were standing was marked out in a peculiar grid pattern. On the perimeters of the grid, surrounding the console, stood seven model obelisks, each about six feet high.

'You already know that the pyramid shape produces huge amounts of natural energy,' Fry said, addressing the TPs from the console, sounding for all the world like a lecturer at a lectern. 'But there is a shape that is even more powerful than that. As far as energy pulses go the most efficient, most powerful shape that exists anywhere in nature is seven-sided.'

Seven obelisks, Megabyte realised. And then he remembered the seven-sided star symbol on Ami's pendant. And the star shape Adam had found in the tomb.

And the seven stars of Amtoudi.

'And it has other powers too,' Fry continued. 'The power to prolong life, for instance – that's why Reece – Rameses – is still alive after four thousand years. He was one of the most awesome people who ever walked the Earth, and he realised that it was within his grasp to tap into this incredible power. That's why he had Tate construct the obelisks.'

'You mean Tate's immortal as well?' Megabyte asked in amazement.

'Of course.'

Megabyte turned to his friends, and gave a helpless shrug. 'Why am I surprised? Nothing should surprise me anymore!'

'Tate erected obelisks in seven different locations in Egypt in a fantastic feat of planning and organisation,' Fry said. 'And once the obelisks were firmly in place all he had to do was to wait for the light . . .'

'From the star system Amtoudi!' Ami realised. 'Of course! Tate placed the seven obelisks to match up to the exact same shape in the sky.'

'The luminosity of Amtoudi's seven suns supplies exactly the light frequency to trigger the reaction on the ground,' explained Fry. 'Rees and Tate built the first, and by far still the most mighty, power generator on the planet. The stars lined up and the energy blasted out, from obelisk to obelisk. The second that happened, Rees focused the energy and caught hold of it – '

'And how did he do that without cooking his brains?' Megabyte asked, but Adam had already guessed the answer.

'He used the Marhaba Stone, didn't he?'

'Exactly! It's made from a meteorite, the densest, toughest thing found on Earth. It sucked in the power like a massively powerful battery. He used the energy in it to make himself immortal and he became the Pharaoh of all Egypt, the most powerful man on Earth.'

'So what went wrong?' Megabyte asked.

'Technology,' Fry said. 'Rameses knew that, like any battery, over time the energy within the Marhaba Stone would grow weaker and weaker. So he placed it inside a specially constructed pyramid.'

'In the hope that pyramid power would make it last forever,' said Adam, remembering what Megabyte had told him of the mysterious preservative powers of the pyramid shape.

'But the tools the Ancient Egyptians had were primitive,' Fry reminded them. 'The Pyramids were magnificent, of course, but they weren't *perfect* pyramids. Over the centuries the energy dribbled away and the Marhaba Stone became lifeless, and Rameses' visionary plans for the future died with it. He was left with nothing except the knowledge that in four thousand years' time the whole thing would happen again!'

'The stars are back in position tonight,' Adam realised.

'But that's crazy,' Megabyte said. 'It would take more than four thousand years for the stars to be in exactly the same position as they were in Ancient Egypt.'

'Exactly. And that's why he moved the obelisks!' Fry said, and smiled at the TPs' stunned expression. 'He hired teams of men to haul Cleopatra's Needle out of the sands at Alexandria and relocated it two and half thousand miles away here in London. He moved another one to Madrid, one to Rome, and one he erected in the Place de Concorde in Paris. Two went to the East – to Budapest and to Odessa. And the seventh one he left right there, guarding the Temple of Karnak in Luxor.'

'It's not possible . . .' Adam said, scarcely able to comprehend the great guile and ingenuity of Sam Rees.

'It is a plan so grandiose in conception, so beautifully engineered, so boundless in its vision it staggers the mind of mortal men in its magnificence!' Fry declaimed, and operated a control on the console. 'Behold the stone shall move! And the stars shall shine!'

Seven beams of laser light spat down from the overhead projectors, striking each of the model obelisks. Energy crackled from obelisk to obelisk, recreating the familiar seven-sided star figure of Amtoudi. Fry threw back his head and laughed triumphantly.

'A new order!' he cried. 'A new order far more glorious than the first will reign forever!'

'We've got to stop this!' Ami said, as she felt the energy from the star-shape increase: the heat it was generating was almost too much for her to bear.

'Turn that thing off!' Adam cried, but Fry ignored him, and turned up the power like a man possessed. The energy was reaching critical: within seconds the whole thing was going to blow, taking Fry and the Tomorrow People with it.

'I was right!' Megabyte said. 'He's set us up again!'

Ami raced towards Fry and ripped open the front of his shirt. There, hanging around his neck, was a star-shaped pendant, similar to the one Ami had worn herself. She wrenched it from Fry's neck, and, ignoring Adam and Megabyte's calls for her to teleport away, heaved it at one of the obelisks. There was a massive explosion, and the obelisk crashed to the ground.

With the circuit broken, the energy Fry had released ran unchecked, dancing around the Tomorrow People and Fry and encircling them in bands of deadly power. But free of Sam Rees' power, Fry briefly came to this senses, and saw what he had done. He tried to adjust the controls on the console, but to no avail. The world was spinning sickeningly around him, and he was rapidly losing consciousness. He slumped forwards on to the control desk, knocking a lever.

The angle of the light projectors altered infinitesimally, so that the beams of laser light no longer shone down on the obelisks. Deprived of a focus, the unchecked energy was dissipated, and sank harmlessly into the Earth.

Megabyte rushed over to the collapsed Fry. He checked his pulse: he was unconscious but still breathing.

'That guy is bad news!' he said.

'Rameses Ak'Hara used him,' Adam said. 'He knew the only way to trap us was if we believed every word Fry said. And the only way we'd believe him was if he told us the truth. He used Felix Fry to tell us everything, so that he could kill us all.'

'That's mean, that is, like, really mean!'

'Come on, guys!' Ami said. 'What are we going to do? There's no time left!'

Adam looked at his watch, Ami was wrong: there was some time left.

'OK, guys,' he said. 'We've got half an hour to save the world. Is that enough pressure for you?'

Chapter Eighteen

Night had fallen as Adam, Ami and Megabyte left the observatory. In the dark and cloudless sky overhead the seven stars of Amtoudi twinkled brightly. On any other night they would have appeared a beautiful sight; today the Tomorrow People knew that they presaged the end of the world.

'What if we just took out one of the obelisks, like Ami did back in there?' Megabyte suggested. 'We could get some dynamite or ram Cleopatra's Needle with a truck or something.'

Adam shook his head. 'You saw what happened – the whole thing went crazy,' he reminded them. 'Imagine that multiplied a thousand times! There has to be another way . . .'

'I'm dying to hear what you're going to come up with, pal!'

'Let's keep calm, and think this one through,' Ami suggested. 'Rameses got Tate to steal the Marhaba Stone so that he could harness the energy from Amtoudi just like he did last time.'

'Except this time around, it's going to be colossal,' Megabyte said gloomily. 'It'll give him more power than all the nuclear weapons on the planet put together, all stored in a hunk of rock the size of a pineapple.'

'But he'd have to build himself another pyramid!' Adam suddenly realised. 'Otherwise what's to stop all the power leaking out of the Stone like it did last time? And now he's got the technology to do it! Computers, modern building materials! He can build a pyramid accurate to a millionth of a millimetre. He can have ultimate power forever.'

'A pyramid in the middle of London?' Megabyte said sarcastically. 'Don't you think that someone might just have noticed? A thing like that is kinda hard to hide!'

Megabyte had a point, Adam knew. But they had to defeat Sam Rees. Otherwise London, the world, the whole of creation would become merely a puppet subservient to the will of Sam Rees; he couldn't let that happen, couldn't let Sam Rees cancel so many thousands of years of civilisation with just one single thought.

Adam looked down at the River Thames, at all the great historical buildings on its bank, knowing that soon there would be no more in Sam Rees' masterplan to reconstruct the world in his image. Soon they'd all be gone: the Houses of Parliament, Saint Paul's Cathedral, even the Rees Foundation Tower, with its huge beacon shining red and gold in the night sky.

There was his pyramid! It had been under their noses all the time! That was where Sam Rees would draw down the power of Amtoudi!

'We need to smash the Stone,' Adam said with determination. 'Then the power would just go out of it and Rameses would be left empty-handed.'

'It's a crazy idea!' Megabyte protested. 'It sounds much too simple.'

'It's not simple,' Ami pointed out. 'The Marhaba Stone is tougher than diamond. Nothing can harm it. How can you destroy a thing like that?'

'I don't know,' said Adam. 'So let's go and ask someone who might!'

'We've been waiting for you,' Millicent said as the Tomorrow People teleported outside her houseboat. By her side stood Red Rainwear, Lizzie Motherwell and Rupert Short, all of them standing to attention like some madcap miniature army.

She strode up to each of the TPs, and hugged them fiercely. 'My saviours!' she said warmly, all trace of her terrible ordeal at the hands of Sam Rees now vanished. 'I knew from the very first time I saw you down by the river that you were the ones Destiny had sent to help us! So to battle, my friends! And quickly too!'

Adam held up his hands. 'No, *we'll* go, Millicent,' he said. 'Just tell us how to destroy the Marhaba Stone.'

'We shall all of us go,' Millicent said, in a determined voice. 'We are an army of peace! We shall march in the face of evil and we shall turn him to the good!'

'Turn Sam Rees to the good?' jibed Megabyte. 'You have got to be kidding!'

'Everything we know and love is at stake,' Millicent said, and by her side Red Rainwear, Lizzie and Rupert nodded their heads in fervent agreement. 'Take us there, and we shall speak to him.'

'Speak to him? And say what?'

'In the darkest of hearts there still lurks a glimmer of light, my dear friend. We must find that light and magnify it.'

'There's got to be something more practical we can do!' Megabyte said.

'Can you stop the Earth from spinning, or the stars turn back?' Millicent asked. 'If you can, then do it. If you can't take us there!'

'It's too late for talking,' Adam said, joining his voice to Megabyte's. 'Smashing that stone is the only answer!'

Megabyte sneaked a look at Adam. 'Go along with them,' he whispered. 'If they all want to go and have tea and cake with Rameses that's great. It gives us the perfect distraction.' Adam and Megabyte nodded their assent to Millicent: they would teleport her and her friends into Rameses' sanctum.

'That's what I call fighting talk, carrot top!' Millicent said, and ruffled Megabyte's ginger hair.

'What's the difference?' said Ami, as she looked up into the night sky. 'We're all going to die tonight anyway.'

Millicent turned to Rupert. 'Sound the bugle,' she commanded, and to the TPs' utter disbelief the tall man took a kid's plastic bugle from out of his satchel and blew upon it.

'Let battle commence!'

Chapter Nineteen

The man known to some as Sam Rees was no longer dressed in his customary grey suit. Now he was wearing crimson ceremonial robes, the kind that, as Rameses Ak'Hara, he had worn over four thousand years ago. He was standing in front of a breathtaking golden throne, a few feet away from the wall, suspended above which, in the claws of the Egyptian stone bird, was the Marhaba Stone. It pulsated with its eerie purple light, as though somehow sensing that its time of becoming was once more at hand.

The shuttered roof had been opened to the night sky, and in the blackness the seven stars of Amtoudi blazed bright and steady. There were but mere minutes to go, Rees realised, before the stars were exactly aligned with the seven obelisks around the world. Mere minutes before the age of mankind ended; and the age of Rameses Ak'Hara was born anew.

Tate, who was also dressed in ceremonial vestments, bowed low to his master. From a little way off, the black-besuited Scully watched, fascinated. He was not the only observer of Sam Rees' coming apotheosis: hidden behind a pillar Adam, Ami and Megabyte were also spectators at the ceremony.

'Everything is ready, O powerful majesty,' Tate said. 'The triumph of your glorious vision is at hand. Nothing can now go wrong. It is my hope that your confidence in me is restored, mighty Rameses.'

Rees regarded Tate, not bothering to hide the scorn and distaste he felt for his trusted aide down the centuries. 'Your mistakes have been many, your deceits inexcusable, your sycophantic fawnings repugnant,' he declared. 'However, in certain respects you have served me well, and for that I shall honour my promise. There awaits you still a place by my side in the New Kingdom.'

Tate sank to his knees, 'I thank you, mighty Rameses, I thank you!'

Scully stepped forward now, ready at last to stake his claim to a piece of immortality. 'And me, mighty Rameses?' he asked hopefully.

Sam Rees seemed to notice Scully's presence for the first time. 'You are of no further use,' he said simply. At his feet his killer cat trained its deadly eyes on Scully – and with a blood-curdling shriek that would haunt the Tomorrow People for the rest of their lives, Scully's body was torn apart, atom by atom, till all that was left of him was a pile of ash and charred flesh on the marbled floor of Sam Rees' sanctuary.

From his hiding place, Adam looked up at the Marhaba Stone, nestled in the claws of the giant bird.

– *We've got to get that stone away from there!* he said.

– *But how?* asked Ami.

Adam pointed to the hieroglyphic symbols which were hewn into the wall, Rees and Tate were busy making preparations for their ceremony, and most of the chamber was in darkness save for the four flaming braziers at each of the four cardinal points. If Adam could use the hieroglyphic symbols as foot- and hand-holds, he might just be able to reach the Stone before Rees saw him.

Rees turned to Tate. 'Now it is time,' he said, and proceeded to the great golden throne below the Marhaba Stone. 'Help me.'

Tate escorted his master to the throne, and, when he was seated, bowed down low before him. For a second Tate thought he heard something and glanced into the shadow behind the throne. Adam pressed himself even deeper into the shadows, willing against all hope that Tate hadn't spotted him.

'I am impatient,' Rees said. 'Begin the ceremony.'

'This is indeed an inspiring moment,' Tate said, his attention diverted from Adam, who began his slow ascent of the wall and towards the sacred Stone. 'We have waited long for this.'

'You find me calm and ready to embrace my destiny,' Rees said, and gazed through the open roof at the constellation of Amtoudi! 'Begin!'

Standing before his lord's throne, Tate raised his arms to the stars and began the incantation that would bestow power absolute on Rameses Ak'Hara.

'Woe to him that assaileth thee, O Rameses Ak'H-ara!' he intoned, closing his eyes and entering a semi-trance-like state. 'Thy city endures, whereas he that assaileth thee is cast down and shall perish . . .'

From their hiding place Ami and Megabyte watched Adam's slow climb up the wall. He was about a third of the way up now, making his perilous ascent handhold by painful handhold. Ami glanced at the Marhaba Stone: was it her imagination or was it glowing more brightly now? Megabyte nudged her and drew her attention to the stars.

A faint trickle of light, like a shooting star, seemed to be journeying from one of the seven stars and connecting it to another. This had to be their imagination, they knew. But then a shaft of light shot out from another of the Amtoudi stars to its neighbour. When they were all connected to each other in the familiar star shape, and linked to the seven corresponding obelisks on the surface of the Earth then they knew that the power would be drawn down to Sam Rees and the Marhaba Stone.

Ami and Megabyte were witnessing nothing less than the beginning of the end of the world.

Tate continued his mumbled prayer, oblivious to all that was going on around him. Adam was almost level with the great stone bird now, but to reach the

Marhaba Stone would mean him leaving the safety of the shadows. If Tate or Rees saw him now . . .

Rees gazed up at the seven stars of Amtoudi, now almost all connected by beams of concentrated solar light; completing the circuit, channelling the energy back and forth between them, ready to be stored into the Marhaba Stone, which even now was soaking up the mighty stellar energies.

'It begins!' Sam Rees cried out in ecstasy, and closed his eyes to feel the starlight on his face. 'The immortal life-force! I hear its whisper, feel its life force blow warm across my soul. It is . . . beautiful!'

Adam was almost within arm's reach of the Marhaba Stone now. Just a little more . . . just a little more . . .

Suddenly the bright blaring sound of a child's plastic bugle cut through the air, and Rees snapped his eyes open, Millicent was standing before him.

'We meet again,' she said.

– *Now's our chance!* said Megabyte as he and Ami took advantage of the unexpected diversion to leave their hiding place, and run behind Rees' throne, ready to catch the Marhaba Stone if Adam was successful in dislodging it from the claws of the bird.

Millicent smiled at Sam Rees, who sat there, flabbergasted, lost for words for the first time in four thousand years. Finally he found his voice.

'Whatever can you hope to achieve by coming here now at this time?' he asked. Also for the first time in four thousand years there was fear in Sam Rees' voice. 'You know nothing in the world can prevent this from happening.'

'*You* could prevent it,' Millicent said.

On the wall Adam stretched out and reached for the Marhaba Stone. Suddenly a blinding flash of light burst out of the heavens from Amtoudi and struck the Stone. Adam almost lost his grip and fell; he swung from one of the hieroglyphs with one hand, holding on with bruised and bleeding fingers.

Rees registered the burst of light, if not Adam's presence so close to the Marhaba Stone. 'You see? It has begun now.'

Millicent glared back at her ancient enemy. 'You will fail,' she stated. 'You will be stopped, and if not by me then by others. Evil is always crushed ultimately. You have lived long enough to know that.'

'Words, mere words!' Rees boomed. 'I am omnipotent! You shall cower at my feet!'

'I deny all evil,' Millicent declared. 'I summon the forces of good to take up arms and do battle with you!'

The sound of a child's bugle blared through the chamber again.

'I condemn you, Messengers of Light!' Rees creid out. 'You cannot touch me! I am invincible.'

Millicent smiled at Rees and reached out a hand for him; Rees had many weapons and she had but one.

'We love you,' she said.

Rees trembled. The remark seemed to shoot through his body, like a blazing spear, Ami and Megabyte watched on, transfixed. It was as though Millicent had opened a gaping wound in the man's psyche, reminding him of the good that must surely exist even in someone as evil as he.

Rees struggled to regain his composure and glanced over to Tate who had been watching the encounter with a mixture of awe and terror. Rees instructed him to continue the incantation, in an effort to exclude all other thoughts from their minds.

'He who exalts Ak'Hara, who magnifies his name, who causes the land to belong to him alone . . .'

Millicent took a football whistle out of her pocket and blew a long loud shriek on it. 'Forward!' she cried.

'Blessed is he who is useful and truthful to Ak'Hara,' Rees continued, and then was aware of a flash of red appearing by the side of his throne. Red Rainwear winked at him.

'Having a fun time?' he yelled and then giggled.

Perturbed, Rees lost the flow of his grand incantation. He began again, but no sooner had he started than Rupert Short burst into the room, bashing on a battered tin drum which hung around his neck.

Suddenly Red Rainwear popped up from the other side of Rees's throne. 'I didn't hear you!' he said. 'I asked you if you were having a fun time!' He took a party blower from the pocket of his raincoat and blew it hard into Rees' face.

Trying hard to shut out the madness, Rees started once again. 'He shall ascend to the Temple of the New Kingdom whereupon the lowly shall bow their heads in admiration . . .'

Rupert had given up his drum-playing, and was now performing cartwheels in front of Rees' throne, making a mockery of his solemn ceremony.

Above them Adam reached out for the Marhaba Stone again. Another bolt of light cracked out of the sky, feeding the Stone. Adam pulled back just in time. He looked up at the sky: the star formation was almost complete. Bands of stellar light connected the stars of Amtoudi to each other: the star shape was now visible for everyone to see. Rees' victory was but seconds away.

A shaft of light streaked out of the sky and blasted Cleopatra's Needle on the banks of the Thames. The bolt of natural energy reflected off the tip of the needle, and, like a Scud missile, went zooming straight towards the pyramid on top of Rees' building, and channelled itself directly into the Marhaba Stone. A similar bolt hit the obelisk in Paris, and was beamed straight to the Marhaba Stone in London.

By now Red Rainwear and Rupert Stone had brought chaos to Sam Rees' sanctuary, a pandemonium which was complete anathema to Rees' concept or order. Rupert was doing farmyard impressions now, and Red Rainwear was dancing a lunatic jig with his unfurled umbrella. Lizzie Motherwell had joined in the fun too, and, overcoming her shyness at long last, had launched into an operatic aria.

Unable to concentrate any longer, Rees turned to his killer cat, who had been hiding in the shadows, uncertain what to do.

'Kill them all!' Rees screeched. 'Kill them all!'

The cat trained its eyes on Red Rainwear, but, before it could fire, a cry of 'Here, kitty, kitty, kitty' made it turn towards Lizzie. And then Rupert caught its attention. And then Rainwear again. And then Lizzie, playing a manic and topsy-turvy game of cat-and-mouse.

And then Rees caught sight of Adam, high above him, reaching out yet again for the Marhaba Stone. 'Destroy him!' he bellowed.

Ignoring Red Rainwear and his friends, the cat spun around and hissed, fixing Adam in its sights. Adam's fingers were just about to reach the Stone.

In the sky overhead, seven bolts of pure white light, reflected from seven obelisks around the globe, converged on Sam Rees' building, homing in on the Marhaba Stone. They formed themselves into a single shaft of light, brighter than a thousand suns, the pure elemental force called into existence by Sam Rees.

As they bore down on the Marhaba Stone, Adam jumped for his life.

At that precise second, the cat fired at Adam, missing him by the barest fraction, and instead hitting the Marhaba Stone, knocking it out of the claws of the giant Egyptian bird.

As Adam was caught by Ami and Megabyte, the Marhaba Stone thudded to the floor, white-hot and smoking. Still greedy for more energy, it attracted tentacles of elemental energy towards it, and, now that it was no longer secured, the bolts of energy made it roll about the floor, this way and that, like a football being kicked along the ground by the elemental forces of nature herself.

Adam, Ami and Megabyte watched on in horror as the fingers of natural energy rolled the Marhaba Stone closer and closer to the throne where Rees and Tate and Rees' killer cat now stood, rooted to the spot with fear.

The tentacles of energy converged once more, transforming themselves into one massive pillar of fire which swooped down upon Rees and Tate. There was a tremendous unchecked outpouring of natural power, which made the Tomorrow People cover their eyes.

When they looked up again, the energy had dissipated. Above them in the night sky the stars of Amtoudi had moved on, their deadly conjunction over, and the star-shape rapidly fading away.

Of Rees and Tate there was no sign, just a smouldering pile of ash. In the centre of the ashes lay the Marhaba Stone, glowing white-hot with heat.

Adam looked at his two companions. 'Everybody all right?' he asked.

Ami and Megabyte nodded, and then pointed over to a spot just beyond the throne. In a haze of green Tutankhamun was smiling at them. He walked over and picked up the white-hot Marhaba Stone.

– *Shokran!* he said, *Shokran!*

Adam laughed. 'I guess that means thanks!'

'Aw, don't mention it,' Megabyte said. 'You're welcome, kid!'

– *Ma'a salaama!*

'We don't know what that means, but *ma'a salaama* to you too!' laughed Adam.

The image of Tutankhamun faded away, taking with him the Marhaba Stone.

Ami was aware of a familiar and friendly hand on her shoulder. She turned around to see Millicent, Red Rainwear, Lizzie and Rupert all smiling at them.

'You did well,' Millicent said proudly. 'And the Marhaba Stone?'

Ami glanced at the spot where Tutankhamun had stood just moments before. 'The boy pharaoh's taken it back to the past – where it belongs.'

Millicent heaved a sigh of relief and winked at her three companions. 'Then we've succeeded!' she said, and Red Rainwear and the others burst into a round of spontaneous applause.

'Thank you, Ami, Adam, Megabyte,' Millicent said. 'We are all so very proud of you, you know.' She looked up to the heavens, at the stars, moving peacefully in their course. Thank you!'

Adam, Ami and Megabyte gazed up at the stars too, overcome by their faraway beauty and mystery. When they looked down again, there was no sign of Millicent or the others. They had vanished from their lives as silently and as mysteriously as they had arrived.

Or not quite. Lying in neat little heaps on the floor were four little bundles of clothes: a red raincoat; a schoolboy's uniform; a milkmaid's costume; and Millicent's rag-bag of scruffy second-hand clothes.

The Tomorrow People stared back up at the stars, and, in the distance, the stars of Amtoudi seemed to look back down, winking merrily at them. Who were Millicent and her friends? they wondered. Where had they come from? And where were they now?

Adam, Ami and Megabyte realised that they would probably never know.

Until, at least, the next time.

Until tomorrow . . .

ZOOL

MEET ZOOL, THE ALIEN NINJA FROM THE NTH DIMENSION

'Cooler than Mario, smarter than Sonic . . . '

Two things Zool is not!
1. Boring . . .
2. An ant. This is a vile lie put about by his arch enemy Mental Block. Ants are small, hard working insects with lots of legs, Zool is an alien from outer space with breath-taking powers. Also ants do not have their names written on the soles of their shoes. And Zool does, so there!

ZOOL RULES
Isbn: 0 7522 0952 3

COOL ZOOL
Isbn: 0 7522 0957 4

MIGHTY MORPHIN POWER RANGERS

The Mighty Morphin Power Rangers are teenagers with special abilities brought together to defend the Earth against an intergalactic sorceress named Rita. Drawing strength from the spirits of ancient dinosaurs, the Rangers also benefit from the futuristic technology given to them by the inter-dimensional being, Zordon.

IT'S MORPHIN TIME!
Isbn: 0 7522 0939 6

MEGAZORD TO THE RESCUE!
Isbn: 0 7522 0944 2

THE TERROR TOAD
Isbn: 0 7522 0949 3

RITA'S REVENGE
Isbn: 0 7522 0954 X

TAKE THAT

Introducing the books every
Take That fan should read!

TAKE THAT – OUR STORY

Piers Morgan

The hottest band in Britain are talented, down-to-earth, funny and hard working. Now, for the first time, the boys have told their own amazing story.

Isbn: 1 85283 839 6

TAKE THAT ON THE ROAD

Piers Morgan

Take That have taken the charts by storm and driven teenage girls mad all over the world with their fresh-faced good looks and slick dance routines. This book takes a behind-the-scenes look at Take That on tour and gives an insight into this incredibly popular band.

Isbn: 1 85283 396 3

TAKE THAT UNDER MY PILLOW

This gift pack of five mini books in a slipcase is essential reading for any Take That fan. Each book is devoted to one of the stars of the band and contains twenty exclusive photographs with their fact files and quotes.

Isbn: 0 7522 0988 4

HOW TO ORDER YOUR BOXTREE BOOKS

HORROR HIGH		
☐ 0 7522 0996 3	*Bad Moon Rising*	£2.99
☐ 0 7522 0971 X	*Rave On!*	£2.99
☐ 1 85283 358 0	*Symphony of Terror*	£2.99
☐ 1 85283 363 7	*Demon Brood*	£2.99
ZOOL		
☐ 0 7522 0952 3	*Zool Rules*	£3.99
☐ 0 7522 0957 4	*Cool Zool*	£3.99
MIGHTY MORPHIN POWER RANGERS		
☐ 0 7522 0939 6	*It's Morphin Time*	£2.99
☐ 0 7522 0944 2	*Megazord To The Rescue*	£2.99
☐ 0 7522 0949 3	*The Terror Toad*	£2.99
☐ 0 7522 0954 X	*Rita's Revenge*	£2.99
TAKE THAT		
☐ 1 85283 839 6	*Our Story*	£5.99
☐ 1 85283 396 3	*On The Road*	£5.99
☐ 0 7522 0988 4	*Under My Pillow*	£5.99
SAVED BY THE BELL		
☐ 0 7522 0990 6	*Zack's Last Scam*	£3.50
☐ 0 7522 0985 X	*Zack Strikes Back*	£3.50
☐ 0 7522 0901 9	*Girls' Night Out*	£3.50
☐ 0 7522 0955 7	*One Wild Weekend*	£3.50
☐ 0 7522 0961 2	*Super Saved By The Bell Scrapbook*	£3.99
CALIFORNIA DREAMS		
☐ 0 7522 0916 7	*Playing For Keeps*	£3.50
☐ 0 7522 0906 X	*Perfect Harmony*	£3.50
☐ 0 7522 0911 6	*Who Can You Trust?*	£3.50

All these books are available at your local bookshop or newsagent, or can be ordered direct from the publisher. Just tick the titles you want and fill in the form below.

Prices and availability subject to charge without notice.

Boxtree Cash Sales, P.O. Box 11, Falmouth, Cornwall TR10 9EN

Please send a cheque or postal order for the value of the book and add the following for postage and packing:

U.K. including B.F.P.O. – £1.00 for one book plus 50p for the second book, and 30p for each additional book ordered up to a £3.00 maximum.

Overseas including Eire – £2.00 for the first book plus £1.00 for the second book, and 50p for each additional book ordered.

OR please debit this amount from my Access/Visa Card (delete as appropriate).

Card Number ☐☐☐☐☐☐☐☐☐☐☐☐☐☐☐☐

Amount £ ....

Expiry Date on card ....

Signed ....

Name ....

Address ....